# The Stone Building
# and Other Places

# The Stone Building and Other Places

## Aslı Erdoğan

TRANSLATED
FROM THE TURKISH
BY SEVINÇ TÜRKKAN

City Lights Books | San Francisco

First published as *Tas Bina* in Istanbul, Turkey, by Everest Yayinlari in
2009. This edition is published in arrangement with Agence Littéraire
Astier-Pécher.

Library of Congress Cataloging-in-Publication Data
Names: Erdoğan, Aslı, 1967– author. | Türkkan, Sevinç translator.
Title: The stone building and other places / Aslı Erdoğan ; translated
from the Turkish by Sevinç Türkkan.
Other titles: Tas Bina. English
Description: San Francisco : City Lights Books, 2017.
Identifiers: LCCN 2017040160 (print) | LCCN 2017041081
(ebook) | ISBN 9780872867512 | ISBN 9780872867505
Classification: LCC PL248.E657 (ebook) | LCC PL248.E657 T3713
2017 (print) |
 DDC 894/.3533 — dc23
LC record available at https://lccn.loc.gov/2017040160

*The translator would like to acknowledge Daniel Beaumont and Aron Aji
for their incisive suggestions on the translation.*

City Lights Books are published at the City Lights Bookstore
261 Columbus Avenue, San Francisco, CA 94133
www.citylights.com

# CONTENTS

# THE

# MORNING

# VISITOR

Dawn came at last. The night had passed slowly, arduously, like a heavy freight train climbing a steep grade. At sunrise, a patch of light quietly appeared on my attic window, deepening gradually. A sleepy sun, the shy, cautious sun of the North, announced the break of day as if fulfilling an obligation. All I could see was a bit of sky framed by the towering trees and the wet roof slanting up at almost a 90-degree angle. Thin, sad branches swaying in the wind, leaves anticipating their decay, shivering. . . like the hands of a beggar, outstretched in vain. The month was August, the season, supposedly summer. I had already surrendered to the hazy gloom of this northern country, my soul submerged in the sea, the rain, and the mossy smell of this city surrounded by water

Somewhere inside the wooden house, the phone begins to ring, and it goes on ringing for a long time. The room's darkness is deceptive — it's after eight o'clock, but still, it's much too early for this place, a boardinghouse for migrants. Nothing is heard at this hour, except snores, sighs, and the wooden house breathing in its restless sleep. In the room on my right, is the Bosnian who takes particular pleasure from showing off his shrapnel wounds to the cold beauties of the North — most of us carry our wounds more privately. On my left is a Russian who makes a living acting in porn films and likes to listen all night to protest songs from a long-gone era. Further down the hall is a red-haired woman whose origin or occupation no one knows; and at the far end is the supposedly Somalian mother, who's actually a Rumanian, one hundred percent gypsy, a freeloader and a flirt who hasn't worked a single day in her life. She likes to brag about how her accordion can melt even the iciest heart. All of these immigrants, each one having arrived from a different land, on a different night, are lost in sleep now, with the bone-wearying fatigue of borders and frontiers. Resigned to a fate they despise, they trust nothing beyond their misfortune. In this shelter of ours, a cloud stinking of alcohol, sweat, tobacco, and filth drifts slowly, so heavy with all the world's excesses and disappointments that on some mornings the echo of light footsteps can be heard inside of it. Maybe it's a lonely ghost, grimy and bedraggled, taking leave of the house,. Or perhaps the red-haired woman has sampled a new lover.

Before the telephone stops ringing, footsteps can be heard coming up the stairs. Slow and tired footsteps at the end of a long journey. They come closer and closer, and then stop in front of my door. After a few, heart-stopping seconds, I hear my name being spoken. Maybe it's my mind playing tricks on me; a hoarse voice asks for me in my mother tongue.

"Yes, it's me. Come in."

The door opens with its usual creak, a moan like the sound of a violin. A short, swarthy man comes in, along with a rush of bitter cold air that quickly permeates the entire room. His sagging shoulders and wide back fill up the room; the door is already closed, as if it had never been opened. My visitor stands still for a moment and then, with the sudden, mechanical moves of a marionette, he turns toward me, his spindly legs barely able to support his body. His face looks like it's been molded from plaster that hardened before the artist could finish his clumsy job. His large nose seems like it has melted and run down between his hollow cheeks, his eyes are nearly invisible in their deep sockets. His wrinkled, saggy, dark-colored suit is far too big for him and looks as if he never takes it off. He quit shaving and wearing neckties long ago. His once thick, receding black hair still bore the scent of the cool, dark night. I was sure I had seen him before.

After a moment he spoke, "I found out you live here so I thought I'd stop by."

Perhaps I should have mumbled a greeting, should have shaken his freezing-cold hand. Maybe I should have been afraid. But there was nothing to fear in this quiet port city. . . Not even death, it seemed. It, too, would arrive exactly on time, just like the trams, neither early nor late. . .

Clutching his topcoat in his pale hands, he scans my room, squinting. As his eyes adjust to the darkness, his gaze settles at first on the bed squeezed under the slanted ceiling. The scrawny mattress thrown atop a woven iron bedframe looks battered by a struggle with dark nightmares that has only just ended. On the table covered with books, glass jars, dirty cups and overflowing ashtrays, a candle stuck in a beer bottle is still burning. My room, dark at all hours of the day, is spacious and almost empty. In the morning, when I stand under the small window and look up, I feel like I'm in a submarine, surfacing and rushing toward the sky. Random artifacts of everyday life are scattered around the room. These underappreciated, unassuming, faithful objects, witnesses of my unbroken solitude, bear the traces of depressing gloom. Everything, whatever I touch, is scarred and bruised. The clothes spilling out of the suitcase are torn and stained, the books heaped on the table are tattered. The water glasses have become cloudy, the pencils and moldy pieces of bread bear tooth marks, like the nicks and holes on the dreary walls. A small mirror hangs above a sink filled with a foul liquid. So much of the mirror's silvering has fallen off that none of these battered objects can see their own reflections, dissolving instead into the murky haze. For my part,

I see myself on the bruised surfaces of these objects. My own bruised skin. . . The thin, gauzy membrane between me and the void, both within and without, bruised and wounded. . .

"These are cold climes, aren't they?" He smiled, his eyes fixed on the electric heater. He had a compassionate smile. "And it's only August."

I looked at his face without speaking. I could see nothing more than a pair of eyes, a pair of endless, pitch-black tunnels.

"Won't be even two months before it starts snowing. First it's a bitter wind that burns the lungs, blowing in from the sea. The layer of ice on the mud puddles gradually thickens, and one morning you wake up to find yourself in a completely white world. Everything is frozen. Buried alive and dreaming of the day when they'll rise up from their coffin of ice."

He walked to the center of the room, toward the rectangular splash of daylight that resembled a startled eye gazing at the ceiling. In his movement, I recognized the restraint of someone who has always lived in cramped spaces; even in this empty room it seemed like he was afraid of bumping into something. Or maybe he didn't want to leave any trace of himself behind. A wan bouquet of light played over his face. And suddenly, I remembered him. His pale skin the yellow of earth, the purple bags under those eyes whose whites were webbed by red capillaries. . . He, too, was among those whom sleep didn't visit.

"But the darkness is more unbearable than the cold. That sun. . ."

He paused and looked at the bright shape on the floor. As if, should he reach down and open that trapdoor, sunlight would burst forth, filling the room. I turned to the window. Green, quivering branches, silvery drops on the leaves; the soft, dreamy dance of shadows on the window. . . The infinite blue that contains and restricts my vision. . . In those rare moments when the northern sun shines, the entire world is transformed, glowing, smiling. But then the clouds return, and the room seems even darker than before.

"You'll see that sun for an hour, maybe two, each day. Around noon, it will appear like a sickly white stain on the horizon and then, before it can climb, it'll tire out. In fact, the real sun will never rise. Its derelict ghost, an imposter, will spread blank canvases instead of days. The earth's light and dark halves will split off, sliced in two."

He stared at the walls, and I did too, scanning those dingy walls that I knew by heart. There, among the electrical cords dangling like strands of hair, among pipes and water stains resembling scabbed-over wounds, a shadow that had lost its human shape looked back at me. His shadow — bigger, and more terrifying than he was, another shadow among shadows. . .

"And that's when your life will consist of one single night. Only ghosts can endure such a night. Albino people, albino trees, a city where ghosts wander. . . That's when the long night of the mind will begin."

This voice. . . This eerie, familiar, mournful voice had spoken to me before, many times. . . Door after door began to open in my soul; I rushed to close them, shivering from the frigid draft pushing its way in. . .

"At any rate, we don't have much time. You have to decide."

I reached for my pack of cigarettes and the candle.

"Decide and be done with it. That's how life is, plain and simple. Breathe in, breathe out. . . Plain and simple."

He cast a sharp, intense, disapproving look

toward the mirror, but all he saw was a blurry, mottled reflection.

"I'll tell you a story that happened thousands of years ago," he began, his eyelids closing slowly like the lid of a coffin.

"I won't listen. You always take me back there. (I was speaking for the first time. Was I really speaking?) You come to remind me that I have never left that place. That dark cell, it follows me wherever I go. In fact, it lives inside of me. It grows like the roots of a tree at night. It spreads and spreads, tearing through my skin to get out, and then it takes shape, finding its outline in the emptiness."

I pointed to my room.

"You can see for yourself, it's as if I keep building the same three-dimensional scene and then locking myself up inside of it. My life is the infinite palimpsest of the same picture. Trees, horizon, sky. . . Wherever I look, inside or outside, I see only a wall. Whatever direction I take, the past or the future, a stone wall confronts me. Maybe it's because I can't face the emptiness that I hide among walls. The void, its endless echo. . ."

"Once upon a time there was a man," he went on

impatiently. "He was a good man, in fact. You know, everybody is a good person. But this man would change at night. Become bad. Do you understand? Words often fail us. This man would turn into his shadow cast on the wall. Maybe it was his wife who caused him to change, since the worse he became, the more she would indulge him.

"In that faraway land, there was a building that cloaked itself in darkness as soon as the sun fell below the horizon. One of the stone buildings that are found everywhere. . . Do you recall? When darkness fell, so did a deep, immeasurable silence. Those who aren't familiar with nightmares worse than death call it the silence of death. But that's because they can't hear the voices inside the silence, the sound of emptiness breathing.

"And when that dreadful darkness descended, the moonlight caressed the iron bars with its white fingers in satin gloves. The moon has a big heart of white gold, flawless. But that kind of heart can't cope with the darkness. Besides, didn't people invent the iron bars to keep their inner darkness from escaping?

"And there were birds on the roof of that dark building. Birds carrying dry twigs to the roof for hundreds of years without rest. Thinking that, one day, they would have finally piled up enough twigs that the stone building would collapse under the weight, crumble to dust. But when night came, a cruel wind would blow, scattering the twigs. Still, the birds would get back to work each morning. . . Are you crying. Why?

"And when that long night arrived, the man would get ready. He would eat his meal always at the same time, wear the suit his wife had ironed, leaving home always at the same time. No one knew where he went. . . He would walk slowly at first, then build up speed — his footsteps feverish, precise, unwavering. On seeing him, the birds would signal one another, sounding warning calls from one end of the city to the other. The pale, tenderhearted moonlight would hide behind the clouds, hoping that maybe the man would lose his way in the pitch-black darkness. But no man would forget the path he follows at night, would he? Listen, it's not over yet.

"And when that shadow man reached the stone building, the screams would be heard. Bone-chilling screams that wouldn't cease till daybreak. . . It was the birds screaming, the moon screaming. . . As a whirlpool of black flames filled the sky, the night it-self would turn into a scream, endless, unrelenting. It would quiver like a gossamer-thin membrane over the expanding abyss, raw and bloodied, torn, ripped, slashed, covered in horrible wounds, which the thirsty lips of emptiness would suck. In the end, it would smash into pieces, strewn across the four corners of the earth. Nightmares and curses raining down on people like stones from the dark sky, wandering like shadows among the sleepers, covering their bodies with black snow, filling the deepest trenches, oozing into the most secret arteries, pouncing like a blind ti-ger, seizing sleep. . . And then would begin the single, long, endless night of the mind."

When I looked up, he had already gone. His let-ter lay on the table. I opened my drawer and placed it among the others. No matter where I went, they found me. The dead wrote to me, to recount things I could no longer remember, calling me to a place I would return to sooner or later. They cautioned me against life, for the sake of which I had been running away from my story. They knew that the future, my elusive refuge, was nothing but the past, recounted time and time again. The only visitor who came to my cell — the dark, eternal cell inside me — was the exiled ghost of the past that awaited me. . . I have not opened even one of the envelopes, but I knew. Inside were dry twigs, pale gold moonlight, and one last, still unclaimed scream. . .

# WOODEN

# BIRDS

The door opened suddenly, and a bright red head peeked in. Dijana's breathless, impatient voice rang out:

"Hurry up, Felicita! Do we have to wait for you all day? Get your fat ass out of that bed. I swear, you're like the walking dead!"

The door closed as quickly as it had opened, shutting out the hospital corridor's smell of disinfectant, Dijana's shrill voice, and her offhand, stinging sarcasm.

Filiz, or "Felicita" as she was called with distinct irony by the lung patients — was an extremely gloomy, withdrawn, and wounded person. With her status as a political refugee, her PhD in history, and the numerous thick volumes she kept in her room, in the eyes of the other patients she was a snooty intellectual. "Ah, our Felicita," Dijana would say. "I'd rather read a book about cancer than have a conversation with her. Getting a few words out of her is like pulling teeth." Our dark and frail Felicita! Felicita, who had been imprisoned in her own country for two years, who had never bothered to look up from her books and learn to speak German without an accent, even after ten years!

Filiz eased out of bed slowly. Her long illness — double pneumonia and chronic asthma — had taught her to use her strength sparingly. She deferred to the moods of her ever-aching, demanding body.

For the first time in six months, she would be leaving the hospital grounds. The name "Filiz Kumcuoğlu" had appeared on the list for a two-hour Saturday pass, reserved for only those patients who'd reached a certain stage of recovery. Dijana, an expert at eluding the night-shift nurse and snooping in patient files — the ultimate adventure of hospital life — had known of these developments since Monday. She had prepared "a huge surprise" for Filiz. THE AMAZON EXPRESS! Filiz had earned the right to share in the secret of the third-floor patients and board the Amazon Express.

Filiz really had no particular expectations. At the most, she thought they'd go to T. village — the only place inhabited by humans within a twenty-mile radius — and get a couple of drinks. Perhaps they would meet the young men of the village, or the patients of the male sanatorium who were as worn out as they were. What else was there to do in the middle of the Black Forest?

As she was heading out the door, Filiz suddenly remembered a story she'd heard at least twenty years earlier and had buried somewhere deep in her memory. At the turn of the century, the female tuberculosis patients of Heybeli Island Sanatorium, would sneak into the woods at night and make love to male tuberculosis patients. Sallow, terminally ill women in white nightgowns, walking with torches in hand... The story probably wasn't true, but she'd thought it was tragically poetic. Her own life was bereft of poetry, and her personal tragedies, by now too many to count, were like leeches sucking the very soul from her body.

*Exit through the double-paned door! Turn your back on the foreboding "T. Hospital, Pulmonary Patients Entrance" sign and walk quickly, looking straight ahead, until you reach the edge of the building's giant shadow. Stand there at the border of the sun's domain, take a deep breath, and then slowly, carefully, take the step that brings you out of the shadow. Suddenly, even the weak northern sun will be enough to warm your back, and you'll believe it's actually possible to erase your entire past and start anew! Let the sun play over your hair, let the forest cloak itself in vivid colors, let the shapes and outlines disappear, let truth become pure light.*

Filiz thought of Nadyezdha, the sad Nadyezdha in Chekhov's *The Duel*, who dreams of soaring to the sky by spreading her arms out in flight. Filiz often felt that she could have been a Chekhov character. Perhaps she could transform into a bird right then and there, but at most it would be a wooden bird. A bird whose wings weren't made to fly but only to make mechanical noises, something lifeless and ridiculous. She was overcome with nervous excitement. Filiz wanted to cry and laugh, live and die at the same time.

"Come on Felicita! You've frozen up like a mummy! We're going to be late."

Joining in with Dijana's cry was Gerda's contralto, hoarse from tuberculosis and smoking: "You'll miss the Amazon Express!"

They were a group of six women gathered at the door. "Three foreigners, three Germans, three tubercular, three asthmatic," Filiz quickly classified them. "All of the Germans are tubercular, while we Third World-ers are asthmatic. Though one would have expected the reverse." Martha and Gerda, the two tall blonde Germans, had managed to remain sturdy and strong, despite their tuberculosis. (In fact, Gerda wasn't particularly tall or blonde, but in Filiz's eyes, indifferent to personal details, the two were identical, and she had pegged them as the working-class women in their small circle.) Filiz was somewhat cowed by their physical strength, their boorish manners, but at the same time she secretly envied their stubborn determination to fend for themselves. The third German was Beatrice, a twenty-year-old with hollow cheeks, thin as a totem pole, an introverted heroin addict. With her short, chestnut-colored hair, her sad eyes that always seemed to be searching for something, and her adolescent's stick-like body, the girl saddened Filiz. Dijana was the trickster, the red fox popping out from behind every rock. She didn't give a damn or get rattled by anything. Except for being called Yugoslav instead of Croat. And then there was Graciela, the Argentinian...

The only patient in the sanatorium who was as isolated as Filiz — perhaps even more so — was Graciela. Unanimously described as "distinguished, elegant, cultured," privileged from birth and quite well off, her presence among the pulmonary patients was an example of life's cruel sense of humor. She was only a little over five feet tall (even shorter than Filiz), dainty and petite. Her straight hair and bangs, her "Marlene Dietrich eyebrows" — which she plucked religiously, even in the hospital — and her almond-shaped eyes, with a gaze as warm as it was icy, had earned her the moniker of "Evita." She was the favorite of the doctors and nurses, who treated her as if she were a fragile antique vase. She somehow made everyone feel that she should be treated delicately. But Filiz had recognized the hardness in that perfectly composed face of a porcelain figurine. Graciela had a smile that frightened people. She reminded Filiz of her primary school teacher, dainty and chic in her scarves, and an expert tormentor in the classroom.

When she first saw Graciela, Filiz had thought she was a visitor who'd mistakenly walked into the patients' cafeteria. Graciela was seated by the window, at a table with one chair. She was wearing a tight, black velvet skirt and a striking blouse unbuttoned to reveal her cleavage. Between her lovely breasts hung a gleaming, heart-shaped pendant. Sheer stockings and a pair of high-heeled, buckled "tango shoes" completed her look. Among the patients with unwashed hair, walking around in sweats and sandals, Graciela stood out like a rare tropical flower. And then one day Dijana, the hospital gossip, had burst into Filiz's room and disclosed a secret:

"You know that Argentinian? Evita is just like you."

"What do you mean 'just like me'?"

"I mean a political refugee. Prison, torture, all the rest. That's how her lungs gave out, in fact. Her ex-husband was a diplomat, both of them came from wealthy families with deep roots and influential friends. But, it turns out, the man stepped on somebody's toes and a warrant was issued for his arrest.

He fled in a matter of hours. Leaving his wife behind. For two months they tried to get Graciela to talk, but she wouldn't reveal his whereabouts. And maybe she didn't know. Can you believe it? That little kitten of a woman?! Don't be fooled by appearances."

This was a devastating blow for Filiz. It felt like a mockery of her deepest agonies, denigrating her personal history, her very being. She had crafted an image of herself as a mythic hero, and only by worshiping this hero could she go on with her life. Her dreadful past, the memory of it, was the necessary proof of her existence and it claimed a sacred corner of her soul. But now that conceited woman had defiled her icons. What right could she have to the same tragedies as the strong, brave, principled Filiz (that's how she described herself), who had paid such a high price for her beliefs? And for what had Evita suffered? The love of a potbellied, contemptible man with two mistresses!

The procession of sick women walked along the narrow asphalt road that twisted and turned like a gray snake on its way to the T. Valley. At the very start of the journey the group had split in two, like a cell dividing. The leaders, Dijana and the two burly

Germans, started up a trivial conversation. A rambling Saturday afternoon conversation on topics of absolutely no interest to Filiz. It began with the usual nitpicking complaints about the doctors — the female doctors were treated with jealousy while the handsome male doctors were flattered. Then they took up the subject of the cafeteria: the food and coffee were roundly condemned, as were the shows on TV. Next, they compared the charms of Banderas and Pitt, with the Germans rooting for Banderas while Dijana — a fan of the Anglo-Saxon race — championed Pitt. Finally, they dredged up a a few random memories from the time before they were hospitalized. . . In the factory where Martha had worked four years ago, a female worker was found completely naked with her throat slashed. Gerda also had a few murder stories in the deep-freeze of her memory, one of which she took out to reheat and serve. Dijana, whose family lived in Bosnia, didn't say a word about violence; she hid behind a silence that loomed like an avalanche.

Beatrice, never quite sure of where she belonged, walked by herself, alone in her inner world. She was trying to drink in, sip by sip without wasting a single drop, the extraordinary September afternoon, the emerald-green valley spreading before her, and the two hours of freedom. She looked happy, and this happiness on her ruined young face was even more moving than a sorrowful expression.

Filiz ended up walking alongside Graciela, and she searched for something trivial to talk about.

"To be honest, it's surprising to see you on the Amazon Express."

"Why?" asked Graciela sharply. A cold flame shone in her eyes — a hint of the molten ore, the anger hidden for years at the core of her being. "They didn't tell you where we're going, did they?"

"No, they're keeping it a big secret."

"It is indeed a very big secret, the Amazon Express." (A mocking, scheming tone of voice, with a smile like a scar.) "Even you will be surprised."

"I'm guessing we're going to the village?"

Graciela brought her finger with its long, cherry-red nail, to her lips. "Shhhh," she said. Like the picture of the nurse on the "Silence Please!" sign back at the sanatorium.

Filiz had neither the stamina nor the desire to continue the conversation. She concentrated on enjoying the walk. She was going to be released in eight months; she was walking in fairytale woods, she was taking in the air, pure and delicious as water. Air that filled her tired lungs, cleansing them of the grime of the past. A tender, generous sun, an infinity of green stretching to the horizon, and the simple, unadulterated, glorious happiness of being able to walk to her heart's content. Unconstrained. With no closed doors in sight. . . Ward doors with iron bars; sound-proof hospital doors with room numbers and lubricated hinges. . . A healthy person would never know the sublime pleasure of being able to use one's legs to carry oneself forward freely. Filiz took note of the forest's incomparable scent. It wasn't as sweet and tame as the smell of the freshly mown hospital lawn; it was raw, primordial, dizzying. Perhaps it was the eerie silence that made her head spin. The T. Valley spread out before her like a densely woven green carpet; it was as though the hills, cascading one after another, were signaling to her. In the valley, where the autumn light had painted everything in sharp relief, sun and shadow were waging an endless turf war. The cross on the village church, gleaming like gold, was discernible from afar. "Everything is so light and carefree, it's enough to make a person feel sentimental," she thought.

Beatrice approached the two black-haired women, her palms full of wild berries. She must have resolved her identity crisis and decided that she belonged among the "foreigners." The tragic bond attracting these two former prisoners was drawing Beatrice in as well, consuming her. Heroin had taught her loneliness, despair, devastation, and although she was the youngest among them, she was the one most intimate with death. She carried death in her childlike body. Others tried to believe in life, to commit to it, to belong, and they were still trying, but Beatrice had already renounced life by the time she was sixteen. Heroin, prostitution, hepatitis, tuberculosis. . . She'd suffered one fatal blow after another, but each time, at the count of nine before the referee could call the fight, she got back on her feet to withstand yet another beating.

"Would you like some wild berries?" (No, neither of them wanted any.)

"On TV last night, there was a program about Argentina. Did you see it?" (No, neither had.)

"They showed Buenos Aires. An extraordinary city. So moody! A bit like Berlin, the architecture, the cafés. . . They showed a neighborhood full of colorful houses, like the rainbow: Labakar. . ."

"La Boca," Graciela corrected her. "Means 'mouth.' The birthplace of the tango."

"That's right. La Boca. The neighborhood of bohemians, painters, and musicians."

"These days, it's full of pickpockets and street peddlers."

"Do you dance the tango?" Filiz asked excitedly.

"No, I'm not from Buenos Aires. I'm from Mendoza."

(Somehow, I was sure this woman was from Buenos Aires and was a perfect tango dancer.)

"Mendoza?"

"On the border of Chile. A city at the base of Aconcagua."

"Aconcagua. The highest mountain of South America!" (In Germany, even the junkies are well educated!)

Silence fell among them. The perfunctory conversation ended abruptly, as if cut off by a knife. As if the three women had absolutely nothing more to say to one another. Then, "Look. There. Look at that rope on the lower branch!" Beatrice couldn't control the excitement in her voice. The two older women looked in puzzlement at this ordinary piece of rope. "A dwarf must have hanged himself here," Beatrice continued, with the livid imagination of a twenty-year-old addict. But then she blushed, suddenly remembering that her walking companions were also quite petite. Thankfully, no one had taken offense.

When the procession of women left the road descending to the valley and turned west, toward the steep hills covered in dense woods, Filiz grew wary. So, they would not be visiting the T. village after all. Perhaps, like schoolchildren or prisoners on furlough, they had chosen an Edenic hideaway for their Saturday freedom. But if that were the case, there would be no need to rush or constantly check the time. The Amazon Express! Did it refer to the rainforests or to those women, the mythical huntress-warriors who severed men from their lives along with their right breasts?

They were no longer walking on a wide, sunny asphalt road, now they were advancing single-file on a difficult trail crowded by roots and underbrush. The true forest journey had begun. Even the filtered sunlight was green. Thorns greeted the forest travelers, irritating them at first, but then becoming increasingly aggressive. Heath, drifts of ferns, brown butterflies flitting among the branches, shy mushrooms hiding in secluded nooks and crannies, a journey filled with autumn flowers. Pearls of rain dripping from leaves, crystals of refreacted sunlight in the wet, sticky moss on trees. . . Seductive side trails guarding the hidden secret of their destination . . .

Filiz had always lived in big cities. She knew nothing about forests. True, she had been at the sanatorium at the center of the Black Forest for the past eight months, but there, too, the forest had remained inaccessible, abstract and mysterious. At night, the darkness that settled over the window like a black bird — the crowing that accompanied her nightmares — was like a hulking, deaf-mute guard who prevented her from returning to her real life — whatever "real" might mean. Now, having walked deeper into the heart of the forest, she was truly seeing it for the first time. This was much more than a simple introduction; it was the sudden encounter of two beings who had been completely unaware of each other's existence. Which is why Filiz was shaken. She was suddenly face to face with a pure, primitive, magnificent, oceanic spirit. It had propelled her from her dusty, sterile, nutshell of a world and bade her listen to the chords of an altogether different existence. The forest had a wild, vibrant, pulsing rhythm. It was cloaked in strange shadows, contradictions, tremors; its secrets concealed by a quivering, gauzy mist. Trees, trees, trees. . . Ancient, solemn, imposing. . . Imperturbable, as if they had seen all the miracles and crimes on earth. Older than time itself. . . They had sunk their roots deep; for them, freedom did not mean propagating far and wide, but growing ever taller on their single-minded journey to the sky.

When they slowed down at the base of a steep slope, Dijana pulled Filiz aside.

"This isn't the time, I know," she tried to catch her breath, pausing a second or two. "But we need to talk tonight. I wrote Hans a letter."

"The last one I wrote. . . that we wrote together, did you send it?"

Once she spoke aloud, Filiz realized how thirsty and out of breath she was. Her mouth was so dry that she had to work to peel her tongue off her palate.

"Of course, that same day. No reply yet. But wait — it's been nine days already. Maybe it got delayed at the post office. Plus, Hans tends to be a bit slow."

"You believe he'll reply though, right?"

Something like lightning flashed in Dijana's amber-colored eyes, and her face clouded over. "I don't believe. I feel it."

About two months earlier, on her way back from a visit to the chief physician's office, Filiz had seen Dijana in one of the telephone booths on the ground floor. Gripping the phone with both hands, she had been talking and crying at the same time. At first, she thought Dijana had received another piece of terrible news from Yugoslavia — it was in one of those booths that a gravelly voice on the other end of a bad connection had told Dijana that her sister had died in Bosnia. But this time the news was different. Dijana's last lover, the tall, clever Hans, had grown exceedingly weary of this tubercular, ruined woman with her wheezy breathing and the bags under her eyes, the depressing hospital visits. Together, Filiz and Dijana had written five letters to Hans, but even Filiz's sensitive and persuasive pen had not succeeded in getting him to write back.

"If I were you, I'd erase him from my mind."

Filiz knew she was being heartless and aggressive, but she was very tired. She was drenched in sweat and terribly thirsty. She could feel the veins pulsing in her exhausted legs. She had no energy to deal with Dijana's troubles.

"You have a heart of stone!"

"There may well be some stones in my heart. But alright, how about we try to make him jealous?"

"In the middle of the woods? If only these trees rained men instead of pine cones!"

"We could insinuate that there's a budding romance between you and one of the doctors. We'll choose someone with features completely the opposite of Hans'. 'A young surgeon,' 'his long slender fingers,' 'walks in the forest under the moonlight,' and so on."

Dijana smiled, quickly recovering her lightheartedness. She certainly had an exceptional smile; it completely transformed her incongruous features. It was unguarded, sincere, and subtle enough to make an immediate and deep impression. Filiz thought she had never seen an expression that articulated happiness so simply.

"I want him back." Dijana's mood seemed to darken again.

Her voice trembled with an indistinct, imploring tone. If she could just prove that she truly desired

Hans, she seemed to think, perhaps some divine justice would summon him back to her. The dark shadow hiding behind her happy-go-lucky demeanor revealed itself only in moments like this. Dijana kept her true self secret, hidden in deep underground tunnels like some monster who mustn't see daylight.

"He'll come back, I'm sure," Filiz forced a reassuring tone, stifling her feelings. She enjoyed neither lying nor talking about men. She didn't believe in love; she couldn't remember if she ever had, even before she spent thirty-three days in a cell filled with blood and screams.

"Dijana! Dijana!"

"Yes, what is it?"

"We're late! We'll never get there at this rate. We need a short-cut."

"Wait, let me catch up. We'll take a look." She ran toward the Germans, her strides shaky.

Filiz sensed Graciela's burning eyes on her back and turned to face her. Their two gazes met — profound, intense, wounded — and a rapport beyond words was instantly established between them.

"If you want to be happy, happy, trust the little girl, the strength of her faith."

Graciela's face remained perfectly still. Had she understood? Without a doubt.

"Have you ever listened to the Brazilian, Paolinho?"

"No, in fact, I know next to nothing about South American music."

Graciela broke into song. This was a sudden miracle, completely unexpected, moving, extraordinary. . . *"Vida e bonita. . ."*

Incredibly melancholy, silken, a melody that went straight to the heart. One that aroused pleasure and pain in equal measure, music that brought you close to death and to life. Filiz's eyes welled up, she gulped to stifle her tears. She never cried in front of others — even when they held a gun to her head — neither did she sing.

"The words mean something like this: 'Life is beautiful, beautiful, beautiful. . . Whether full of sorrow or happiness, it is, it is beautiful. . . No shame in wanting to be happy . . .' Paolinho was born on the street, he lived in poverty, and died of tuberculosis at thirty-three. I'm telling you all this so you don't just reject the song."

"If someone at the bottom of the abyss tells me that life is beautiful, I should obviously stop and listen. But to truly understand this music one would have to have experienced a different kind of suffering."

Dijana slipped between them. "Listen Felicita, we need to take the short-cut. We have very little time left. Can you handle a mountain path that'll last at the most for twenty-five minutes but is sort of a killer? How are the bellows?"

"They haven't started complaining yet. But I don't understand, what are we late for?"

"That's the whole point: not knowing where you're going until you get there. You have to decide now whether you'll come or not, because we can't just leave you halfway up the mountain. And, as I'm sure you'll agree, we can't carry you on our backs, either."

"I'm coming. I don't turn back half-way."

"Come on girls, Felicita is in! The Women's Squadron! Forward, march!"

Shouts, jokes, and commands rose up from all sides. " Amazon Express, we're on our way!". . . "*Aventa!*". . . "We may die, but we won't turn back!"

"Good God! The hysteria! What a farce!" thought Filiz. "So now we're playing soldiers. A half-crazy caravan of tubercular women. All we need are the bells on our saddles! Oh cruel world, and we can't even breathe. . ."

Shouting loudly, creating a ruckus, the Women's Squadron started up the mountain path. The inhabitants of the woods scampered off, the birds grew quiet, and nature silently withdrew to clear a path for these noisy, reckless, selfish animals. Dijana, who knew the route well, led the pack, moving quickly, deciding their course, finding the trails like a native tracker. Close on her heels followed Martha and Gerda with their broad shoulders. Strong, dependable, confident shoulders. . . The two of them climbed with heavy, sure steps, clearing branches, breaking trails like Panzer scouts, shouting directives to the rearguard. Beatrice was a wild cat just escaped from captivity. Confident and full of energy, she was an agile hiker, thanks to her long legs, her hiking shoes, and above all, her youth. She paused often to extend a hand to her dark-haired friends in need.

Filiz spent the twenty-five-minute journey through the woods drenched in sweat, grabbing at thorny bushes and roots, anxiously searching for solid rocks to set her feet on, nearly fainting from panic and worry. She would occasionally slip on pine needles and fall, or stumble over roots. The brambles escaped her grip, leaving rosy scars, while her body was whipped by branches . Her seldom-used, flaccid muscles began to vibrate like a tuning fork, and her legs felt like heavy sacks full of water. Fits of jaw-rattling chills coursed over her back like cold snakes. She had soaked through her underwear and could not stop thinking about how excessive sweating can be deadly for a lung patient, especially one who had been given her first leave only that day. She could hear the eerie whistle — called the "fog horn" in hospital slang — starting up in her lungs. She cursed herself for having joined this adventure, for senselessly jeopardizing the health that had cost her untold trouble to regain On the verge of weeping from fatigue, remorse, and desperation, she appealed to her personal god, as she would do in times of trouble, praying sincerely, imploring him again and again.

At last, like all terrible things, like physical pain or prison, the journey came to an end, and Filiz was able to look up from the trail and see where she was. Throughout the dreadful twenty-five-minute ordeal, with each step a matter of life and death, she had been trapped in her body, buried in fear, and had paid no attention to her surroundings. Only now — panting, with a tightness in her chest, blinking back the burning salty sweat from her eyes — she saw that they had reached an extraordinary place.

They were standing atop a steep cliff, its face covered in human-sized shrubs and a tangle of tree roots and heath, a vast, spreading net of wild flora. Forty or fifty meters below, a raging river was rushing furiously, thundering, crashing over the jagged rocks it had nicked and carved over time. A path dotted with purple flowers resembling large carnations laced along the horn-shaped ledge right before the river took a sharp turn and disappeared among the rocks.

"A path of purple dreams," Filiz thought.

"We're going down, Felicita. Be very careful."

Filiz scanned her companions, baffled. Everyone looked wretched. Their faces, flushed to a purplish hue, were sweaty, grimy, full of scratches. Their hair was soaked, their shirts, come undone at the waist, were drenched, too, their nipples discernible.

Everyone had fallen again and again, getting cut and scratched all over. What were these women after? What was the point of all this exertion, danger, injury?

"Listen, I've had enough! As if it wasn't enough that we ran through the forest like lunatics, now we're climbing down into that gorge! What is going on here?"

"Don't be a spoilsport," hissed Dijana. "You promised you'd come with us till the end."

"I promised nothing."

"Let her do whatever she wants." This was Martha; no, Gerda.

"Filiz, please tough it out a little bit further. Believe me, it'll be worth it." This was Graciela.

"Come on, please Filiz." Beatrice took her arm, gently pulling it.

"Come on girls! It is 3:23! Seven minutes left!"

Suddenly, the group forgot about Filiz. They began tumbling down the slope like pinecones set in motion with the flick of a finger. Down to the very last drop of their strength, the women grabbed at branches, rocks, whatever they could find, most of the time sliding on their butts, holding hands, helping one another. One false move and they could fall, be torn to pieces. Filiz, too, had become a link in the chain without thinking twice. She submitted to the urgent momentum and joined in the descent down the narrow, slippery line between life and death. The danger stimulated her, arousing all her senses. She was filled with an urge akin to sexual desire. How deeply she loved life right now, feeling the joy of existence in the very marrow of her bones. It wasn't simply a rock or a bush that she grabbed onto with her hand but life itself, the wounded heart of the forest, of earth, of life. A tree bent at an angle almost parallel to the river appeared in her path. It had spread its roots like an octopus over solid rock, managing to grow on this steep slope with stubborn persistence. Its shadow fell on the gorge. The tree extended one of its tired arms to Filiz, and for a brief moment they held hands before they each returned to their own crooked path through life.

After a descent that felt like a journey through the circles of hell, they arrived at a completely different world. Friendly trees, dreamy flowers, all traces of life had vanished; here there were only rocks, terrible, cold rocks. . . Much larger than they had appeared from above, they rose to the sky like shiny black daggers. And then there was the terrifying roar of the river, its blind, aimless anger. . . Filiz had the thought that she had joined up with a troupe of mechanical dolls whose springs had wound down, landing them all in this spot to perform their obscure roles.

Before her startled eyes sat Dijana, on a rock as wide as a double bed. She had assumed a pose common to cheap erotic magazines. Her knees bent slightly, her legs spread wide, she placed both of her hands on her crotch. Her face assumed a pre-orgasmic expression of sexual pleasure. Nearby, Martha was reclined with her profile turned to the river; one of her knees drawn up, she had her head tilted back, clasping her hands behind her neck. Her face, too, wore the expression of a vulgar prostitute. Gerda was on her hands and knees, displaying her magnificent ass. Beatrice was standing, one foot resting on a big rock, her body leaning forward, arms outstretched. She rested her cheek on her knee as if leaning against a tender and passionate male shoulder, her dreamy blue eyes gazing at the water. Confronted with this astonishing scene, Filiz searched for Graciela with one last shred of hope, but she had already joined the performance. Like a statue of a goddess, she stood on a sail-shaped rock — alone, unmoving, half-naked. She had stripped off her blouse and, her right hand resting on her waist, she was pushing her breasts slightly forward. Her pose made Filiz think of a dove; natural, innocent, and fragile. Between her raspberry-colored nipples, stripes of burn marks showed under the silver necklace. She had her eyes fixed on a point up in the sky. The thin fingers of her left hand wandered over her lips — half-open, taut with thirst — as if she couldn't speak, couldn't find words for her intense, painful longing. Her entire body, grown thinner, taller, had become an arrow aimed at the sky, about to be released to hit its mark. Filiz had landed in a mind-boggling dream from which she could not awaken. But even dreams held more meaning, more inner logic than this.

"Felicita, come on, give us a pose. Find something funny."

Filiz remained as stiff as a Sphinx. She understood nothing. Gerda's watch beeped at precisely 3:30. At first, nothing happened. During a minute that slowly evaporated into the mist, the women waited, almost without breathing, in those ridiculous, absurd poses. Then, a canoe appeared among the rocks. The four young men, as was made clear by the badges on their life-jackets, were members of the rowing team of H. University, located seventy kilometers away; strapping, healthy and strong, these athletes were rowing with all their might, exerting superhuman effort to avoid crashing into the towering rocks along the narrowest and most dangerous passage of the river. They spotted the women. Where they had seen them every Saturday.

"Hey you, forest fairies! You again? We're going to drop by your village today!"

"Girls, come on! Show us a little more!"

"We'll tie up the canoe and come back. Don't leave!"

"Hey, Red, what's the point if you don't take off your pants!"

The women didn't respond at all, they didn't even giggle. Stiff and frozen, they were more mute than mechanical dolls.

Whistles, catcalls, jokes about what's "down there," but nothing too vulgar. . . A couple of comments about Beatrice's skinny body, Dijana's shamelessly open crotch, Gerda's ass, Graciela's naked breasts. . . Felicita had posed as herself, motionless, not a thought in her head, remembering, feeling nothing, unable to shift her eyes from Graciela's scars, and the breasts she offered up. At last, as the canoe was about to disappear from view, Filiz's arms slowly lifted to the sky. They spread out rigidly, haltingly, like the wings of a wooden bird that had never learned how to take to the sky, but then they fell, exhausted, collapsing upon her head. One atop the other, like broken wings. Graciela's otherworldly voice rose, wavering, among the river's roar and the receding shouts: "*Vida e bonita. . .*"

Two warm tears, born in the deep wellsprings of Filiz's eyes, ran down her cheeks like two muddy yellow streams, leaving their tracks behind. The canoe had long ago disappeared. The women were alone again in the middle of the forest.

# THE

# PRISONER

She woke up long before the alarm went off. As if checking to make sure the night was over, she opened and closed her eyes a few times in the humid, pre-dawn twilight. She had slept for a total of three hours, and the night — full of tossing and turning, and dreams burdened with an intense realism, much more painful than reality itself — had felt like it dragged on endlessly. A sense of waiting with no beginning and no end...

For hours she had lain like a chained ghost with

her knees pulled up to her belly, afraid to move, pricking up her ears at the slightest noise. Unable to cry, unable to sleep. . . Without lighting even a candle in the darkness. . . The objects in the room, as if in sympathy, had been restive through the night as well, stirring imperceptibly in troubled agitation.

Moved by an inexplicable sense of responsibility, she jumped out of bed. The cold of the house overcame her, numbed her, helped her to not think of anything, anything at all. She went about her daily routine: Brew some tea, empty the ashtray, splash your face with ice cold water, reach for the cigarette pack! The smoke warmed her insides with its sly tenderness — a feeling resembling happiness! Suddenly, seized by a sharp nausea rising from the depths of her body, she remembered the day waiting in ambush. Everything, all that she tried to keep at a distance, crowded into her consciousness. She hurried to the kitchen.

She opened and closed the drawers, the cupboards, noisily, rummaging through the shelves. She had finished the cheese pastry and biscuits she'd bought yesterday. Even though she knew the refrigerator was almost empty, she searched every square inch of it. She found the jar of honey left somewhere at the bottom. With a child's appetite, dipping the stale slices of bread into her tea, she ate them along with the honey. She was neither hungry, nor full. "What an emptiness inside!" she said, rubbing her belly. That's when she remembered the baby for the first time.

Usually, every morning as soon as she woke up she would imagine the baby in her belly, believing that the baby was imagining her in turn. . . At times, she was satisfied with a simple, clear image, say, a college-age girl with a bright smile, her hair tossed by the wind — a proof of life's invincibility and resilience. At other times she'd imagine a miniature human — a stain in human form — with perfect little hands like she'd seen in the ultrasound. Most often, though, she'd imagine a magical, cloudy mirror that freed her long-lost youth from the grip of time and carried it forward, into infinity. The image was of one without out a care about the future, someone who no matter where she might look, sees only the familiar, not the unknown. As if until now she'd never had a future, even when she was young, when she'd had only her useless youth. For the first time the future was being formed, gradually growing, taking shape in flesh and bone. . . A warm being stirring into life; feeding on interrupted dreams as much as it was fed by her own bloodstream. . . A state of waiting with a definite beginning and an end. A miracle. "I am expecting a baby," she would say at every opportunity, anywhere, to anyone she happened to meet. . . As if she didn't completely believe it herself.

The room, crammed with things collected from here and there, from acquaintances, from second-hand stores, struggled for air under the cardigans, blankets, and piles upon piles of newspapers. The dust that had accumulated for weeks made this always dim, small, basement apartment look like an ancient tomb slow-ly being swallowed by the sands. It was as though this place, where she had spent three cold, lonely winters, still belonged to no one — it reflected nothing of her life, offered no hint about her past. Photographs, trin-kets, vases, objects that might trigger memories, she avoided these things as if they would burn her hands. This was her way of denying her womanhood. She hid old letters — stamped "Read" — in a Chinese box in-laid with red and black swallows. As if these letters had been written to be saved forever, to be read again and again, awaiting a time when they would all be framed and hung, like a voice resonating from the walls, pained but never complaining. . . When she felt strong enough she would open the letters, taking sustenance from them as though they were a serum she would later replenish with her own blood. Each time, a bit more.

The night before she'd ironed the only available skirt and jacket she could wear — the dark green set she'd bought her senior year in college. The chair, with her jacket draped over its back, resembled a bow-legged, sulky civil servant. She wore the light green shirt with a scalloped collar — was it called that? — purchased that same year; an ill-fitting slit skirt, too short for her thickening thighs; and a pair of blunt-toed, short-heeled, brown boots that hid the run in her nylons. Completing her look was the chic coat her sister had sent from Stockholm years ago, a couple of sizes too big and looking almost new, since it hadn't been worn in years.

*Wake up the puppet, shake the dust off her, drag her in front of a mirror. Wipe the traces of tears from her face, put on her everyday stone-faced mask so she's ready to appear in public. Cover the deadly paleness with powders, eye shadow, and layers of color, or else you won't pass in the world of humans.*

Her appearance was painfully incongruous in

spite of the color coordination she had accomplished after much deliberation. . . Her hair, which she'd washed at midnight, but couldn't dry because of the power outage, was fuzzy with random curls, resembling a wig left over from the previous century. She turned on the fluorescent light over the mirror, held her breath, and looked at her own face.

To be a woman meant taking on an appearance acceptable to everyone. It meant shouting constantly, "Please, someone, see me!" "See me and turn me into an image to remember forever. The way I could never see myself." On days when she had to dissolve into the crowds, she painted her cheeks and eyelashes clumsily, covering the circles beneath her eyes, drawing jerky lines across her trembling eyelids. As if drawing her own caricature. . . She watched with feral satisfaction as the singularity of her face receded further with each crude brushstroke, the step-by-step erasure of her self as an anonymous woman emerged in the mirror. It was as if she was seeing her legs exposed through the slit in another woman's skirt. She removed the last residues of authenticity by plucking one by one the bristle of blond hairs on her chin, deriving an unexpected pleasure from this pain.

She dried her hands on the blue towel — so soft, as if infused with lotion. This was the only object of his that she still kept. A towel from Bursa, bought at a discount. . . warmer, more intimate than all his passionate caresses or the memory of those caresses. It was still here this morning, it hadn't disappeared — the common fate of objects that bear witness to human loneliness — it had remained, always within reach, waiting. Its mute resolve, its deep-blue-sea softness recalled not so much the man who had left it behind as his absence; and strangely, that feeling seemed to grow with each passing day. "I bought it at the layover," he told her while rummaging in his tiny bag on that night when he had turned up after so many months. "I thought maybe you wouldn't even have a towel in your house." "I have a dozen," she responded, hurt. . .

The doorman had forgotten to leave the paper again. He never remembered the woman living by herself in the basement apartment; sniffing out vulnerability was an ancient instinct. She grabbed her hat and put it on before slamming the door behind her. She climbed up the stifling, dank staircase lined with melted candles, and like a somnambulist, she walked toward the main street, through the alley whose potholes, cracks and bumps she knew by heart.

Shimmering drops were all that remained of the storm that had pummeled the city throughout the night. A colorless, bright spring sky stretched overhead, cold and indifferent as an empty mirror, a narrow span between temporary horizons. . . The city's face, rising straight up in front of her, was wet, tired, quivering with metallic iridescence, shaking itself awake and coming to life. The last rain clouds were passing, slow and sad as a funeral procession.

She walked without paying attention to the muddy puddles, aware of the tapping of her heels as she hurried, placing one foot in front of the other with a steely determination. . . Repaired, renewed, filled with energy. . . Raspy car horns in the distance, an engine refusing to start, a garbage truck, a drill penetrating a metal surface. . . The non-human voices of a world remaking itself each morning. . .

Soon, an odyssey would begin to the offices, highways, workshops and schools. The city's foot-soldiers, still drowsy with sleep, would fill the sidewalks, following a dream they wished would never end. Faces, anxious, abstract, tense, muted, angry. . . Bodies moving through the streets with the restlessness of bridled horses cutting trail over rocks. A tapestry of thousands, tens of thousands of destinies, ambitions, desires, dreams, struggles, crisscrossing, twining indifferently, becoming snarled into a Gordian knot. . . They would haggle, clash, fight without mercy to claim a role in the plot of another, to snatch a share of a world that had long ago been divided up. The only evidence left behind would be crumpled tissues blowing in the wind.

Streets, muddy sidewalks, crowds, others. . . The night had finally ended; the day — even the yearning for another night — had begun, and she quickly disappeared into the city.

She gave a start, as if whiplashed, when she caught sight of her face in the glass. Her rouged mouth resembled an open wound. Bloody, overbearing, obscene. . . She could not stand her reflection and moved away, walking to the window streaked with rain. Electricity was being restored to this neighborhood; the frosty, whitish, fluorescent light suddenly illuminated the café, blinding the eye like a belated winter sun. She was the only customer. The younger of the waiters, tired of watching the woman with a suspicious, condescending gaze, began covering the tables with burgundy tablecloths, securing them with clothespins on each corner. In her fussily assembled outfit, with her legs crossed, she sat as if she were in a display window. He skipped her table, leaving it without a tablecloth. The other waiter was staring absently at the TV, looking as if he'd awaked from hibernation too early and was still unable to collect himself.

'I wish I'd ordered a double,' she thought, drinking the cold, sugary last sip. 'Look at me, just an ordinary woman sitting by herself! Didn't they even notice I'm pregnant?' "Could you refresh my tea, please?"

There was nothing in the papers to occupy her mind. National politics, international politics, exchange rates, the arts and culture calendar. . . The LIFE section. Another new war, with its economic, political, historical causes, the usual colonialist powers, the oppressor and the oppressed, the master-slave dialectic. . . She was only interested in the photos of women. Stylish, attractive, as if infected by a chronic youth-beauty virus, women looking at the camera as if facing eternity. They never ate, drank, wore or said anything that wasn't beautiful. In the flagrant comfort of a life free of tragedy or foolish mistakes, they held forth on human relationships. Fearless, never blinking, they looked directly into the lens. . . They, too, were retouched. One must learn to think positively; if you can't change the world, change your attitude. You should love humans, but you need to forget about them; own this life, claim it for yourself, the dying are always the others anyway. A crossword puzzle hint: an egg-shaped instrument. Her horoscope promised a day full of social activities but she must refrain from unkind acts. A very young woman photographed doing her warm-ups — stretching her long legs on a staircase — complained that she couldn't find true love. (Try substitutes, darling!) She grimaced and closed the paper. She was surprised to realize how spiteful she had become toward the real world — if you could call it that — which she could neither reject nor join up with.

"I had asked for tea," she said in a voice that was louder, more jarring and demanding than she had intended. . .

(Again, she had managed to be ignored.)

"Yes, *abla*, once the water boils!"

Unable to wait any longer, she opened the package and ate the fresh cheese pastries and buttered buns hastily, as if stuffing them into a trash bin. This was the only way she could subdue the emptiness that gnawed at her like a wild animal hidden in the deep recesses of her body.

A noxious smell saturated the dirty yellow walls, the tiled floor, the stained drapery. Under the "No Gambling" sign was an algae-ridden, bone-dry fish tank. Two or three empty porcelain vases, framed newspaper clips, a painting with a view of the sea, a console radio — probably vintage sixties — covered with lace had rendered this dull, spiritless space more human than her own house. She felt gloomy. Her gaze settled on the model ship; the best ones used to be made in prison. Gunshots on the TV startled her.

Suddenly she wanted to bolt from the table, to get outside and run away. Since she'd become pregnant, she had been visited with increasing frequency by an urge to walk away without looking back. Once, transferring from one bus to another, staying no more than a night in any one place, she had traveled for five days and five nights. In fact, she had intended to go back to her hometown, to see her mother; she wouldn't have mentioned the baby, since she planned to have an abortion as soon as she returned to Istanbul. Instead she had found herself stuck at the bus terminal with her ticket in hand, unable to take "that first step" that initiated every journey. For hours. . . Double tea, another double tea, missed buses — there was always another bus — a Nescafé with milk — no milk, then with cream, another cigarette. . . Five days and five nights like this, crossing each city from end to end, drawing circles around cities she passed by and quickly forgot about; noisy, stinking terminals, announcements, tea cups and ashtrays being filled and emptied time and again; sunless, whitewashed, empty motel rooms. . . Until the onset of nausea.

Now it was almost over, that horrible, simply horrible nausea, the retching that emptied her guts out every morning. . . Her oversensitivity to smell, her sore nipples. . . She was hungry more often and never actually felt full; she tired in an instant. But her skin was flawless, fresh, a youthful blush colored her cheeks, making her sharp features, her severe expression, agreeable. This winter, she felt the cold less than she had in previous years. A sense of dedication, holiness, and responsibility that she'd never experienced before. But then again, she'd gone back to smoking.

The waiter approached with slow, haughty steps, his eyes fixed on her lips. As if he wanted to ask her something, but didn't have the courage. Or maybe he was involved in his own private game. She remembered the Chinese box inlaid with swallows, the stamped envelopes, the letters that went on for pages and pages, declaring a war on silence. Airless letters scented with dust, ash, mold, dried blood. . . As if those traces of ink on paper — carefully chosen words, declarations, exclamation marks, semicolons, et ceteras — hadn't been painstakingly drawn, one by one, with a ballpoint pen, but rather, as if it had all emerged spontaneously, through some fissure. How detached they were, those letters, in spite of their sincere, eloquent, message of love! How calm and ordinary in the context of so much pain, loss, and tragedy! As if they were reaching out not to her, but to unhearing multitudes, to vacant mirrors on the horizons. And yet she, above all, was someone willing to hear, to listen, to take it all on. . . What stayed with her after reading and almost committing them to memory, was an oppressive heaviness, a sense of suffocation. . .

And beyond that, the heartache! Their relations were rooted in words crossed out by prison censors, words she labored to exhume one by one, like a gravedigger. In what hadn't been said more than what had, under the censor's thick, coal-black stripes. . . The waiter grabbed her empty glass and walked even more haughtily back to the tea stand.

Perched on the edge of the world of humans, sitting there in her dark brown coat, she looked like a pleasant but not very well-executed painting, as if she belonged to a bygone era, a long-forgotten time. Her gaze — aggrieved, inaccessible, clouded — had lost the capacity to see, gaining in its place a faculty much sharper, much darker. She examined her yellowish, swollen fingers and unpolished nails. Her acquired identity had taken over, altered her posture, her manner of sitting, her expression. She held her back straighter, smoking her cigarette by pressing her lips out elegantly to inhale, relaxing them to blow the smoke away. But the transformation only served to reveal the woman hiding behind it, deepening the melancholy coiled like a black snake in the hollows of her eyes. In her outdated clothes from ten years prior, a skirt that was much too short, and her fuzzy curls, she presented an odd, touching, cheerless figure. Her face — made up in its blotchy paints — was completely naked, altogether broken. Her chapped, nervous lips quivered now and then.

Hers was a deep, dark, agonizing loneliness. It always attacked from the most unexpected place, from what she thought of as the most inaccessible part of herself: her memory. She had watched over her loneliness, tended to it, nursed it with her own blood, and in times of despair, it would feed her in turn. She was like the wrapping that protects a mummy from disintegration, but she couldn't keep love, no matter how tightly she bound it, from rotting from within. Love was nothing more than a collective unknown. An echo she couldn't be sure if she heard in the spreading silence of her ability to remember. Love was replaced by memories, memories that were refined, repaired, and perfected; memories that consumed her, down to the very marrow of her bones. . . Reignited over and over by the weary breath blown over their ashes, until they were memories no more. . . A crystalized anguish and longing, a desire that burned in the most remote parts of her body.

"What's that movie called?" the drowsy waiter asked half-heartedly.

"I forget!"

"Was it good?"

She looked distracted, pensive. Smoking cigarette after cigarette, scribbling on the pages of the newspaper. . . Her eyes fixed on her blurry reflection on the tabletop as she gazed inward. . . This outward appearance was a lie, a sleight of hand, a temporary effect, a fragile shell to keep her from being scattered far and wide when the inner eruptions occurred. Without it, her true self would have collapsed to the floor, leaving black streaks behind as it crawled on its knees to escape. ("But, to where?")

Outside were trees, streets, forgotten seas. Crowds, shadows fell into one another: the others. . . The stone building stood there, like a mountain. Solid, colorless, deaf, dark. Shuttered windows, soot-covered ventilation ducts. . . As if dozens of eyes were looking down through lids sealed shut, weighing the world of humans. She felt sick to her stomach — her stomach, her heart, her soul. . . She bit her lips. As the taste of lipstick reached her tongue, her eyes began to burn.

A dizzying tug of war had taken hold over her body: between what was lost and gone forever and what hadn't yet begun, what belonged to her completely and what did not. Something she couldn't name was growing insistently, unstoppable — a wild, savage, magnificent something; as if she were being forced to grow along with the baby. Kicking out its independence and giving away none of its secrets, the baby wanted to *be*, and wanted it more with each day that passed. To be somebody, to be itself, to be everything. . . As soon as this being saw daylight, all on its own, it would take the irreversible leap into a world where it could fill its lungs to bursting. In a bloody pool of its own making, it would be born.

She had condemned someone else, her own child, to life, knowing too well she would be unable to protect it, either from the truths of life and death, or from their lies. . . Who could protect anyone anyway? She was handing down her tragedy — her own creation of thirty-two years, and passed from generation to generation. Hadn't she refused, in the end, to abort the baby in order to connect to the world of humans with a thin, immortal, unbreakable cord? In order to let loose a triumphant cry against loneliness, to cast the long chain of her anchor as far as she could toward the unknowable harbors of the future? So that, in time, she could exist in her own story? She tailored a heart for the unborn child from her defeated, wounded heart; a brand-new face from her own intolerable face. . . Now no one could knock her down, trample her, destroy her. Perhaps this was her message in a bottle, sent to the mirror on the horizons; to everything she had lost, to everything she was going to lose, to experience, past and future. . . A child. A decision deferred; an irreversible light that seeped through her skin, into her womb; hope and regret, a fluke. Its hands had even taken shape, perfectly formed, a miraculous stain in the shape of a human. Very soon, 'I am alive,' it would say, 'I am not a mummy. . . I want life itself.'

"Here's your tea. I apologize, but it just finished brewing. . ." The young waiter was standing right next to her, too close; she couldn't tell if he was being polite or mocking her. The smell of soap emanated from his hands. There was a lure, a provocation in his notably swarthy, thick, rough wrists. He wasn't fond of words — he rounded them as if chewing cud, spitting them from the corner of his mouth.

"I don't want it anymore," she said, raising her eyes from her reflection on the table full of fingerprints. . .

"I'm sorry, what? Well, but. . ."

"I don't want it anymore. Please bring me the check." She looked up at him, her hands folded on the table. The waiter hesitated for a moment, looking at the dark, wet shadows under her eyes. Had she been crying? He turned his back to her, a back too young, strong and attractive to be worried about such caprices.

She leaned back, taking a deep breath. She looked out at the street like an actress observing the stage she was about to enter. The buses were running busily, the bus stops filling and emptying in turn, lines forming in front of ATMs. The city's day of social activities was about to begin. Everyone seemed to be sufficiently content. With themselves, with everything. . .

Now the streets were filled with women peering at display windows with shrewd, calculating eyes. . . Masters of bargaining, they determined the fate of this noisy, angry world. They had talented fingers; their breasts were firm under their bras. They gave birth, they breastfed, raised children; they kept their houses stocked with all kinds of cheeses, they had framed pictures, porcelain vases for their flowers; they never hesitated in showing their claws to waiters, doormen, and above all, other women. Authentic tragedies, losses, humiliations, they bore them silently as if keeping a secret, convincing themselves that their suffering was not in vain. They held on to life with long, colorful fingernails that concealed their defeats. With a saint's patience they scraped and scraped, then licked the stardust smeared on their hands with the impatience of a goddess. (While she, all she wanted was an opportunity to prosecute life — if only she could find a single witness . . .) Were they really happy, these women? She folded the paper — she had filled its margins and corners with kites, arrows and clumsily drawn female faces — gathered her belongings and closed her purse. She wiped her eyes, leaned down to adjust her nylons and straighten her skirt. She looked at the stone building. Massive, gloomy, solemn, it stood there waiting. It hadn't dissolved into the night or oozed into the darkness like tar. Unshakeable, untouchable, unassailable. Still, like anyone who takes it upon himself to be God's messenger, it couldn't hide its worldliness. Which made its commands all the more unbearable. To read a death verdict from a drawn straw. . .

In the yard trampled by countless footsteps, but with not a human trace to be seen, a bitter wind was swirling. Ominous, accursed, haunted. . . It made the trees shiver, scattering papers, plastic bottles, men and women who were hard to tell apart. The crowd, subject to an inexorable, relentless will, rushed toward the building as if caught up in a fishnet being suddenly pulled from the water, then quickly fell into line before being swallowed up by the doors in twos and threes. Now, let them struggle, leap, climb onto each other's back as much as they wanted! The stone building simply ground up everyone trapped in its net. Countless lives, years, seasons, hours, dreams and disappointments, hopes and regrets. . . The time was up. Not yet! No. Now.

She left a good tip and headed for the door. It was as if time, dammed up by a logjam all night long, had finally burst through, and now its rushing floodwaters dragged along everything in its path. The clock's second hand had switched sides and was on the attack, forging ahead. 'Calm down, girl,' she said to herself, 'calm down, my baby! Don't abandon me!' She felt as though her entire body was trying to roll itself into a ball; as if she could not get a breath through her parched throat. In front of the stone building, grinning and baring its gums, she felt vulnerable, like a lone bug that had just sprung out from the safety of its shelter. She rubbed her eyes, adjusted her skirt, and walked slowly, gracelessly. As if she were dragging along a massive tail.

She remembered the egg-shaped instrument: Ocarina!

"She forgot her hat," said the young waiter.

"Who?"

"That funny woman who sat by the window for hours."

That night she dreamed of a marsh that extended from one horizon to the other. Reeds taller than a human, scraggly plants with long tangled arms, trees that shivered like old women with brittle limbs. . . Giant vines, low clouds that almost touched the earth. . . A man is running with all his strength. . . Plunging through the mud, staggering, lurching, running, running away. Covered in blood and mud. . . The pack of barking dogs grows louder and louder, the snare tightens. Hopelessly, he lifts his head, as if praying, cursing or in vain defiance, perhaps he wants to look up at the sky for one last time. He sees the ladder descending from the clouds. A ladder made of giant, translucent raindrops like diamonds — an unexpected gift from the heavens. Climbing, he begins to crumble, disintegrating into a thousand specks of light raining down on the earth. That is when the Woman becomes visible. The Goddess of the Marsh. She emerges from among the dead, groping forward through dark waters. Buried to her hips in the mud, she lets her roots sink deeper, down into the earth's memory; moss, dead leaves, leeches hang from her hair, her eyes become food for marsh creatures. She hides the man beneath her skirt, hides him inside the warm, soft, viscous clay. As the night presses on, the dogs and the hunters leave. A terrifying green glow of thousands of poisonous eyes — instead of stars — illuminates the swamp; the air trembles with thousands of trails suddenly lost; nothing is heard but the wheezing of the wind. No one could pass the night here. Other than the Woman. . . She belongs here. This is her true world, this wind, this silence, this terrifying green. The swamp night where the dead and the living call to each other, where the darkness of the earth is inseparable from the darkness of humans. The swamp night that embraces the wayward, the lost, the defeated, whispering visions of underworld rivers. . . Silently, under the pale moonlight, her flesh ripping, ripping, she brings the man back into the world. Smeared in mud and blood. Something has gone wrong — she has birthed a monstrosity with arms for legs and legs for arms. Shaking himself off, the man resumes his escape, trying to run on his feeble arms, falling to the ground and rising, writhing, crawling. . . The woman extends the ladder she has braided from her hair. "Take this road," she tells him, pointing to the path opening across the dark waters, created by her ponderous, muddy tears . . .

She stopped in the middle of the sidewalk. Standing upright and still, like a statue of a goddess at the edge of a cliff. Exposed to all blows. Her face devoid of expression, her gaze fixed. Staring at an imaginary horizon, with eyes no longer able to see, turned into dried-up wells, clutching her purse tightly against her stomach. Her voice was lost, she could not speak. The wind blew her hair about, swaying her body as if she were a cypress tree. She could now set herself afire on the edge of the abyss, let her smoke disperse. She had turned into a defiant call, into a prayer: COME. 'Show yourself to me even for a second, even just once! I cannot go back to that long, painful waiting. To that emptiness. . . I cannot bear it any longer.'

She remained like that until the prisoner was taken from the stone building and carried to the prison van. Upright, inscrutable, mute. Blown by the wind. . . Exposed to all kicks. She saw all of it. The brief light in the man's eyes — bewilderment, joy, gratitude, or love, or none of these; the slight movement at the corner of his lips, the almost imperceptible farewell gesture of his hands cuffed on his chest, his thumbs bending, pointing to the ground — right then the guard pushing the man violently, swearing — his head hitting the metal frame as he and the others were shoved into the vehicle. . . She saw it all.

Even long after the prison van disappeared, she stood there, stock-still, rubbing her brow as if her own head had been smashed.

# THE

# STONE

# BUILDING

# The Beginning

The facts are obvious, contradictory, coarse. . . And blaring. I leave the facts, like a mound of giant stones, to those who busy themselves with important matters. What interests me is the murmur among them. Indistinct, obsessive. . . Digging through the rock pile of facts, I'm after a handful of truths — or what used to be called that, these days it doesn't have a name. Lured on by a flickering light, what if I were to dive deeper and deeper, if I could reach the bottom and make it back — I'm after a handful of sand, the song of the sand that slips through my fingers and disappears. "Those who speak of the shadow, speak the truth." Truth speaks through shadows. Today, I will speak of the stone building, the one that the narrative has avoided at all costs, or at least kept at a safe distance, looking out at it from behind words. Constructed long before I was born, it's five stories tall, if we don't count the basement, and there are steps leading up to the entrance.

One must write with the body, with the naked defenseless body beneath the skin. . . Yet, words only call out to other words. You take the letters "L" and "F," a couple of vowels, "I" and "E," and you write: LIFE. The only key is not to confuse the order. Misplace a letter and you turn the living clay into simple inert matter — as the legend goes. . . like in the legend. . . Life, as I write it, belongs to those who can grab it, with a deep sigh, not with a mere breath. Like plucking a fruit from its branch, a root from the earth. . . As for you, what's left is but an echo, like the hum of waves that you hear when you hold an empty shell to your ear. Life: a word imbibed and consumed down to its very marrow; the hum of a wave of quiet grief, an oceanful of waves.

A young boy once said, "Better to outdare life before it outdares you." He was a reckless soul, a cross of one kind of darkness with another, he had come to know the stone building too early in life. He was never afraid again, either because he remembered that first fear forever or because he forgot it altogether. . . Ever since, they say, he laughs for no apparent reason.

Suppose, on the street leading to the stone building, there's a coffeehouse, and in front of it, winter or summer, a man. (Inside the building, a vast courtyard, surrounding the courtyard, staircases with wire mesh reaching high overhead. . . To keep people from jumping. Because for the past century or two, human life has become too precious to be hurled against the stones. And outside the building, spiraling up to the fifth floor, is a fire escape. At night, under the pale moonlight, shadows appear, climbing up the stairs, but, to this day, no one has been seen climbing down.) The man, like a relic from some forgotten era, is always there, on the sidewalk. . . When he can find them, he sits on newspapers, cartons, cardboard boxes. Around him, you can see empty bottles, food scraps, vomit, puddles of piss. His face, divided into uneven halves by a deep scar, as pitted as the surface of the moon, reveals nothing, not even his age. Still, if you follow the scar like a mountain path over his battered skull, you will arrive at the melancholy hollows of his eyes and find yourself standing at the edge of an abyss. One that speaks not in a human tongue but in that of the wind, moonlight, and rocks. Because you cannot dare ask for his name, you assign to him the first letter of the alphabet: A.

The coffeehouse regulars lead such simple, ordinary lives that any attempt to describe them ends up sounding artificial, forced, exaggerated. In any case, no one here talks about himself much, and even if he did, nobody would listen. Although they've had more than their share of calamity, failure, and humiliation, the regulars still believe that humans are naturally good, though they can't quite explain why there is so much evil on this earth. Each one, in his own way, has come to grips with life — with poverty, with privations, with disappointments called "life." By clenching their fists, by cursing, by humoring each other, by stealing, struggling, and above all, simply by making do. . . Truth be told, they don't have many options. Still, even Hell isn't so bad all the time — even in Hell there's a cup of tea, a corner one can claim as one's own, a friendly gesture, a smile, a familiar song.

Suppose there's a nameless bar across from the coffeehouse where only an exclusive few are allowed entry, where experienced bouncers stand at the door until dawn, showing the drunks and troublemakers to their taxicabs. For the bar's regulars, the lives across the street are stories they'd like to tell one day. Each time they begin inventing a human story. . . (isn't the art of story-telling, in a way, the art of stirring coals without burning your fingers?). . . it leaves behind the bitter taste of death. When they grow weary of this rotten system — the heap of filth that passes for a system — and of the clockwork labyrinths of their souls, they look outward with one final hope. Past their own reflection on the bright window, to the shadowy, silent, indistinct alleyways. . . the courtyards, coal cellars, tunnels, secret passageways where the ghost of freedom roams, rattling its chains. . . They walk as if the streets belong to them, with noisy footsteps, leaving deep footprints, going up and down stairwells swept clean by others. Sometimes they feel entitled to what they desire; at other times, they enjoy the privilege of cruelty, so long as it's not overdone.

After all, who would turn down a life of adventure and strife? Besides, they've paid a princely sum, endured plenty of loss. They've never hesitated before coming to blows, fighting the fight, looking danger in the eye. They've spoken out — with giant capital-letter words in which they could see their own reflection — yet they've expected nothing in return from the indifferent world. When they've had their fill of despair, of stories, crimes, sins, confessions — each one the same as any other — they leave the back alleys behind and revert to their destiny, picking up where they left off. To invent the hell of human freedom — moving beyond good and evil. . . far from absolute good and absolute evil, in the comforting safety of mediocrity. . . After all, every human life is a defeat, but some defeats are more spectacular than others.

Those at the coffeehouse know this hell intimately, even if they don't give it a name. . . "Freedom" reminds them of a yard fenced with wire mesh. As for being "human". . . Isn't one born a "human" with the sound of the very first cry? Still, it's difficult to bear being human, even more difficult to be no more than that.

As for A. . . No one notices him. He lies in front of the window like an empty sack, as he does in front of every door the world slams in his face. The streets belong to him, but he goes nowhere. As if he's captivated by something inside — maybe the stove, or the TV... Something he has worn out by staring at it... The dirty window reflects back a picture of his existence. Tainted, very tainted... His existence is a long poem about being human.

Sometimes, what little life is left in him, that tiny spark, blazes unexpectedly, and turns into an outburst of dark laughter. Wave after wave of uncontrollable laughter making him keel over in convulsions; he manages to raise himself, but, unable to stop, keeps on laughing. The hazy halo of madness can't protect him from cold, pain, hard knocks, but it does protect him from the earliest memories of the stone building. He is known to laugh even when he gets a beating, as if he hasn't cried since the day he was born. (After all, sadness is a luxury not everyone can afford.) He makes no attempt to understand the world — I think I try to do that for him. He doesn't get angry either... He is in the world like a sponge thrown into dirty water. And the world is in him... Caught in his gaze, it wastes away, is hollowed out, turns to simple clay. Well, what is this thing called "life," other than a murky image on the windowpane! Tainted, very tainted, a long poem on nothingness. Speak a little A., withhold your shadow from the words. Give them enough shadow, make them speak the whole truth with the weight of shadows!

I will now defer my laughter and take you to the stone building. When you turn the corner, you'll think you have come to a dead end but the path curves left just in front of the stairs. You will stop there and bid farewell to the world of humans. The path that brings you here will never take you back. Inside, lights are on, day and night; in the stark, ruthless light, all forms — inanimate or human — and their shadows become equal. A fate summarized in a few sentences ends up being the succinct answer one gives to all possible questions. A confession. A confession extracted every hour on the hour. Human: the oldest riddle, matter that speaks.

I loved somebody once. He left his eyes with me. Since he had no one else to leave them with. Love. A word I found by digging through what spills over from the heart, through so much darkness. Nobody had told me "Everyone kills the one they love"! We were together at the stone building. I listened to the voices, listened and waited. When it was my turn, the sun had not yet risen.

You don't believe me, you think I saw the stone building in my dreams, don't you? But aren't we all created from the yeast of dreams? Sooner or later, the day breaks, blood-red streaks appear on the eastern horizon. . . Stars harden in the taut, motionless sky, dispersing one by one into the unseen. The last star lets a rope down, toward us, so that the silent night, the slit and bloodied words, the dispossessed shadows, the impassioned, unwanted dreams, the winged dead, might grab onto it and climb up. . . so that all the dreams that came to live among us and left without goodbyes, might climb to the furthest reaches of the sky where everyone and everything disappears. . .

You don't hear me, do you? Perhaps I shouldn't have told this story in the past tense. I began the song in the wrong place again, and in the wrong key.

# The Humans

A. never managed to finish his story — the rings of hell are more tangled up than a human life. . . Days passed, seasons changed, but he kept his orbit around the stone building, drawing circles that waxed and waned. He walked and walked, and walked again, till he collapsed from exhaustion on the sidewalks, on life's worn-out paths, on its dusky edges. . . His twisted form coiled in front of unyielding doors; shivering in puddles of mud and piss, he told and retold his story. Laughing in the wrong places, laughing more and more... He couldn't find even one person to listen to him. That's why A. learned to speak with the dead, with the birds, with the wind...

When I saw him last, his head was bowed, as if he couldn't bear its weight. His hair covered his forehead and eyes. What frightened me most was that he might lift his head and look at me... What frightened me most... And what I most wanted: for him to look up, see me, murmur a word. A sign, a reproach, a farewell... He did none of these. This is how he left his eyes with me. Since he had no one else to leave them with.

Then, I recognized your voice, my own voice coming from you. How strange! What frightened me most was that you might cry, beg, collapse. You did none of these. As if death were some kind overly dramatic end — a literary device kept on reserve for me. But you stood fast, suspended in the middle of a sentence where the dawn never arrives. The glow of your eyes the color of ash... You lit the last candle of your strength and offered it to the break of day.

Your head had fallen. Covered in the wads of tissue they had plastered to your wounds, it was as if you had arrived at some strange blossoming. Your eyes were like two solitary stars concealed among the branches. You left them with me. I parted the branches one by one. Parted them for days and nights, for years. By the time I had finished, you were already long gone.

## FROM THIS SIDE OF THE WALL

The wall that separates you from yourself is cold and wet, riddled with holes and covered with words carved by thousands of hands, erased by time and by another thousand hands. Fingerprints the color of dried roses. Keepsake roses, faded and pressed after their brief season of bloom, that shower of crimson buds, twisting vines and thorns. Your own voice speaks to you from the other side of the stone wall. "Are you there?" it calls to you. "Don't you worry, we won't stay long," it says, consoling, calming. The voice reminds you of the lullabies your mother used to sing, but it sings them now like a supplication, or maybe an elegy. It wrests words from the prison of language, words to lean on and stand tall, words to light like a candle in the darkness, words to hold in your palm and caress. The thicker the walls, the wider the reach of your dreams. You walk the skies, the meadows, the seashore, the waters, you walk and walk and walk. Your imagination, a pack of wild horses, must gallop, in a frenzy, faster than the whirlwind that had sucked you up and flung you out against the rocks. It turns an ominous stain into the eyes of someone once beloved, into a tree heavy with fruit, into unspoiled forests, continents. Into deserts and oceans, into caravans, into ships whose sails fill with the breath of your soul. . . Into endless stories — color after color, image after image. . . Stories that won't reach the far shore, won't make it through the night. . . It is your imagination that finds a vast universe, molds it from nothingness, only to return it back to its birthplace, nothingness, as the day begins to dawn. A world the color of pure light meets your eyes. If you want to open them. Later, when that voice that calls to you — consoles you, cries in your name, seeps into your night — when that voice, too, goes quiet, then, even solitude vanishes into thin air.

When I saw A. again, he had grown dark, a man darker than dark. It was a summer day, in the early hours when daylight hadn't yet taken on any color. Hunched in front of the stone building, he was sitting on the worn-out sidewalk wet with morning dew. It was as if the night, in its hasty departure, had left behind this odd-looking, half-blind bird, perched there on the sidewalk, alone and completely ignored, for he was too strange for anyone with human senses to notice. Even the daylight seemed oblivious to him, leaving him in the shadows as it lit up everything else. He spoke in a slow monotone, never raising his eyes from the ground. Every so often he'd shake his head, insistently repeating something over and over; then he'd look uncertain, puzzled, as if he'd lost his place, only to go back and start over. Now seized by a fear of words, now soothed by the sound of his own voice, he spoke nonstop. His purple veins stood out, his face, a dense, impenetrable forest, was completely still, as was his body aside from a soft swaying from side to side. But his fingers were in constant motion, pointing, folding, unfolding, endlessly kneading an invisible ball of clay. Words were like tiny loaves of stolen bread, he hid them in his hands, kept them warm, breaking off large chunks, giving them form one by one. It was a rambling speech, now rising now falling, never quite finding an endpoint, fitful, circuitous, full of dead ends. It was more of a story or a fable than a grievance or a discourse. A tale about the precarious human condition. . . Maybe he was writing a letter to life with invisible ink, or merely adding footnotes. Taking up the most shunned, the most battered words, he was trying to pull together the scattered pieces of his being, patching the gaps with newspaper, replacing what had been lost forever with random castoffs, stitching together a soul for himself — or something others would call a "soul" — from the world's trash. A. was speaking with the stones, with the sidewalks saturated with the night's chill and desolation, with the soil buried under the pavement. . . The roots of trees twining with the dead — victims with their assassins — the memory of the soil, of fire, iron and ash, woven through the painful labor of rebirth. . . He was exhausted, too exhausted to even take one step toward our common world spinning in its orbit. He seemed to have shrunk inside of his loose, sagging jacket, with his baggy pants falling from his waist, and yet, even this emaciated body was too heavy for him to carry along. His shoestrings were missing; his arms and legs, which he couldn't move, hung from his torso like dead branches. The streets belonged to him, but he went nowhere. There he stood, in front of the stone building, swaying unconsciously, like an eyelid closing, opening, then closing again. Like a scar from an old burn on the earth's skin, like a birth mark. Like a wax seal — proof of authenticity — bleeding out along the edges when pressure is applied and then hardening into its final shape, its human shape. He was amazingly calm — he had understood everything, forgiven everything. His brows were knit, his eyes intense, his placid voice was serious, almost emotionless, except, in rare instances, when a nervous tremor convulsed his muscles, his body shaking as if burning with fever, and a dark wave swept through his face, wiping away any trace of life, his eyes going dark, like two burnt-out stars. As if he was pulling out a nail, or tightening a screw into his heart, he managed to make himself whole in his story, to give birth to a seedling, achieve an arduous flowering. And then he would fall silent, lifting his arms as if to say, "This is how life is," like a hopeless, sullen jester at the end of his act, waiting for the crowd to applaud. Still, it was the language of wounds that spoke in him, of wounds and desolation, of deserted marketplaces, streets, beds in a jail cell, of stories with no protagonist. . . A language that no one wants and no one hears, made of words wrested from silence, wrapped in an aura of inscrutability, and returned to silence. If it could have been heard, it might have called to the human world like the Siren's song, luring it in and smashing it against the walls of the stone building. If someone had been there to look into his eyes — eyes that had long ago given up on seeing — they would have seen mirrors reflecting the world's deluge back at the empty mirrors of their own vacant stare, receding all the way back to the moment of their own creation from simple clay. But these days A. spoke only to the stones, to the soil — its silence — hidden beneath the stone. . . He wrote his letter to the wounded dove that had settled on his shoulder and fallen asleep. To the wind and to the dead. . . A. spoke through empty hands that held his life, divided by a scar into two unequal halves. He expected no response. At the end, he began to laugh with an unbridled terrifying cackle, as he retreated from his own story. He extracted his name from the alloy called life. Dredging himself from that colossal, unintelligible tableau, he set the world free, floating like a blank sheet of paper in the dawn of a new day.

꩜

You listen to the sounds, whispers, footsteps, screams, the calls of the world outside, its endless drone... The world outside that has had you erased from all its pictures for a long time now. The sounds and echoes carried generously by the stones — are they real, are they memory or illusion, you cannot tell... Heels tapping along, doors slamming, a telephone insistently ringing somewhere, and no one answers... A scream, it stops, turns into a moan, starts again. This time, it persists. A scream that builds like an avalanche, forcing you to retreat into darkness, all the way back to the walls. Does it belong to a woman or a man, human or a creature much more innocent, you cannot tell. Is it coming from the body or the soul itself? From the unfathomable past that you mean when you say 'my body' or 'my soul,' or from the future lost to you in an instant? Maybe it's the cry of the Sphinx hurling itself into the abyss. And you prepare yourself too, as much as you can... You decide which of your you's to send to the battlefront, which ones to call back. One of you will most certainly be terrified. You weigh what you can give up and what you can't, close whatever accounts you can close. Like an aspen leaf, another body trembles in the recesses of your body, and the walls of the stone building tremble along with it; and the vast world and the stars that encircle it tremble along with it, too. You embrace your best possible you, bidding a hasty farewell. Are you ready? it asks with a quiet, nocturnal smile, are you ready to turn into a winged creature, into a fern forest, into a stone? A stone as ancient as this world, resilient, mute, pocked. . . If you wish to be reborn, you must be buried with a mirror and a heart. But your heart has become a gauzy membrane around a void. If you wish to see your own face, you must cry a river. A muddy, subterranean river that will show you in whose image you were made. Are you ready to fly? I don't know. *Take this one to the fifth floor!*

Alone, you straighten up in your body, your exhausted arms hang limp like broken wings. You stand beyond hope and despair, beyond good and evil. Your last place of refuge. The awareness hits you like a blast of cold air, eternity is on the wind blowing through your hair as if to make you whole again, piecing you back together, returning your face to you. Fingers of moonlight caress your eyes thirsty for sleep, showing you life as a miracle, then gently lower your eyelids. Your body, immune to wounds now, quivers like a taut bowstring, standing at the earth's gate, awaiting its final banishment. It only takes two heartbeats, your journey from one horizon to the other; the morning star, your star, lets down the rope for you to climb all the way up to it; for the first time, acutely aware of your innocence, you lay your head down on the thorny night. Alone, defeated and proud, you lay claim to all the fates that converge here. Swaying quietly in the wind, standing fast in the middle of your own disappearance, you take responsibility for the lies of life and death. One more time, one last time, the magnificent song of the chorus is heard. It begins gently, expands, wave upon wave, rising beyond all the world's sounds and silences, beyond its skies and nights. Calling out to you, calling out to you and your solitude in your most authentic voice — that remote, improbably magnificent chorus, drums of victory or defeat, that wind. . . The wind.

# The Stones

I think I was talking. As if I would have collapsed to the ground if I stopped for a moment, and then even the stone surface would not have kept me from falling deeper. Outside, the sun must have been setting. I was still quiet, calm, collected — yet there was no longer a subject to which I could attach these adjectives. The experiences weren't mine. I wasn't there, inside my own life. We are human, I was saying between the lines. You know, like the honest man that

Diogenes went in search of, lamp in hand, street after street, the very last one that some wanted to summon, others — if they were to find him — would keep him alive, or kill him. It's an unfortunate twist of fate that we find ourselves on the opposite sides of desks, papers, locked doors, of light and darkness; it's an unlucky twist of fate. Otherwise, we're essentially the same, each of us a victim. And maybe I wasn't saying these things, but stating my address, place and date of birth. Suddenly, in the middle of my sentence, as if someone had called my name, I turned around and noticed the outside door was ajar — and no matter how much I tried to figure it out, I couldn't recall when it had been opened. Seized with terror, I closed my eyes for the duration of a brief but infinite fall — and I wish I had kept them closed for much longer. They materialized as if in a dream, surrounded by tall wire mesh fences, bare walls, stones, in dimly lit underground corridors. . . Half-concealed in the shadows, they seemed even more dreamlike. Leaning on one another, they walked slowly, ponderously. . . Pausing, stumbling, shuffling along. . . As silently as if they were under water. As silently as their elongated shadows dragging along the floor behind them, breaking at sharp angles on the stones. Their souls were saturated with this silence. Even from a distance, I could see the agony in every step they took, almost with superhuman effort, like they were walking over broken glass. The insuperable agony contorting their childlike faces, bending their backs and spreading cell by cell through their limbs. . . Their bodies bore the marks — chalky, ash colored, ruby-red, deep purple — left by the blows, by thirst, by cold. They were too exhausted to take a single step. They had emerged from windowless rooms, underground cells that sunlight never reached, from among shadows and that kept the secret of screams. Rising through the seven layers of the earth. . . They had emerged at the border of the seen and the unseen, young, silent silhouettes carved from darkness. Step after excruciating step, they walked slowly, arduously, as if shackled and dragging an immense burden. All of them had wounded feet. The oldest among them — he was sixteen or seventeen years old — had a broken leg, clumsily wrapped with a filthy cloth from the knee down. Without a cane to lean on, he held onto a boy who was close in height. As if caught in some cruel, endless game of hopscotch, with the stone being placed forever farther and farther ahead, he hopped along in agony — his teeth clenched, his face twisted, his cheeks quivering like feeble wings. The procession passed by without uttering a word, heads bowed, gaze frozen. For a moment I forgot where I was. I thought I was in a field hospital behind the battle line, among soldiers returning from combat. A battalion of the wounded, approaching slowly, shouldering their dead and trailing loose gauze and bandages. Covered in mud, in defeat, in the congealed, black blood of waiting in ambush, these were the children of the stone building. Emaciated, weak, if not yet beaten to death then beaten black and blue again. Guilty children who had taken over the crimes committed for generations, who were more accustomed to cold and degradation than we were, whose bones heal faster. . . They were the children of ruthless streets, of deserted marketplaces, of cell beds, of mugshots impossible to tell apart, children who didn't die off easily, whom tragedy deemed unworthy, a few of whom we could perhaps 'reform'. . . They had come from desolate valleys, from swamps, from the dark dreams of the underworld, quietly appearing at the border of the unseen. From a distant solitude, like the middle of a desert. It was as if they had been walking for months, for years, and would be walking for months and years to come, on a loop longer than a human life, on cobblestone roads of silence, along life's edges, its dark nights. In the Gordian knots, at the crossroads of our human existence... Shouldering our humanity as they carried the corpses of their own youth. The spirit of our times hung from them in tatters — our haphazardly mummified collective spirit — trailing gauze and leaving deep, dark tracks behind. Their limbs entangled like branches in springtime, their gaze frozen, the throng advanced without uttering a single word. Perhaps exchanging a silent nod, a secret, a curse, maybe a reassuring "hang on" at times, then a "let it go"... And as they passed by, the world exhaled and grew altogether quiet, still and silent as a mirror, watching its crippled children, those it could not bear to look in the eye. Out of the blue, one of them began to sing, his voice barely audible. The tune was familiar but I couldn't understand the words, and perhaps they had no equivalents in the world of words. It was as if he was sharing a morsel of bread, a morsel he had hidden among the crumbs in his pockets. They joined him immediately — one taking up the simple, steady refrain where the other left off, voices gradually rising. They were singing to live, passionately singing in the name of life, giving it their all, whatever they still had left... A momentary gleam in their eyes — youth's pure, dazzling flare, still coming through, despite everything... An artless song catching fire in the dark and quickly turning into a blaze — the last candle of their strength. An unintelligible, relentless, spellbinding song... Rising from the earth, from a place they had barely known existed before, from the earth's most desolate, inaccessible place — a heart gripped in ice — the song swelled up, overflowing, renewing itself in all things, re-creating the skies even among the stones. Wave after wave it spread, filling every heart in its path with the melancholy of night, the pull of infinity. Such joy — at being alive — unlike happiness or hope, such unfettered love... The song kept rising and rising, with every person who heard it, extending beyond the last yellow line of sunset on the horizon. To the place it had been calling out to all along, to an unclaimed heart, Nobody's heart, in the nether regions of the sky. Along a path where everyone, everything is lost... Like a shooting star vanishing into its own night.

The chorus I had been dimly hearing was nearby, at my door, within sight. Coming closer, more real, more grounded, more me. They were singing the Human song, in its utter desperation and splendor; and the very moment that I recognized its melody — we all do, what we don't recognize is our own voice within it — is when I slipped through life's fingers. Like an 'E,' insignificant by itself, I slipped and fell through the L's, the I's, and the F's. I broke apart beyond repair. Countless I's, distant, lost, deaf to one another... I would never be leaving the stone building.

A guard had lined up the kidnappers, pickpockets, carjackers, the juvies, all the petty criminals who had tasted the bastinado, and he was walking them to the latrines. One of them suddenly started a song in a language I didn't understand, and soon the rest joined in. The voices grew louder and louder then stopped. They disappeared into the dark hallways as quickly as they had appeared, swept into an eternity of bare walls, stones, wire mesh fences taller than a man. Shadows, young, mute, dark — the chorus singing that extraordinary, enchanted song that I still can hear, that I still seek...

You crawl on your belly over the stones grey as sorrow, in the desolate, cold hallways of memory, from one end of the wall to the other, then back. . . You crawl between the endless nights and days of limbo, between sky and earth, between flames and ice. . . In narrow rivulets of blood, dried-up or still flowing, silenced or never silent. . . The distance between two horizons is the span of a wall. You wander among the ruins, stumbling like a ghost whose eye sockets are packed with dust; your body hangs like tattered rags from your bones; time, its very essence disguised as nothingness, ascends your spine; your jaws chatter. You bite your tongue until you tear away the last word. You crawl on your knees and elbows toward the invisible river beyond the rocks, doubled over with thirst, your lips parched and bleeding. . . Dreaming of waking up in the open sea, of having been long dead. . . By now you must have figured out the meaning of the song that comes through the walls, from the depths, the very depths. "Let me go," chants the chorus of young dead, chanting it over and over, and nothing else. . . It's unbearable; you bang your head against the walls like you're knocking at the door of the earth's heart. . . At least the stones are merciful; they spare you your own image. You've discarded your half-naked body — as if you ever owned it — left it behind like a shell that's been cracked open. Word by word, you've dripped out of your own story; clot by clot, like a used placenta you've been strewn across the endless stony night. You have no place else to go. These stones, this wind arriving from quiet corners, carrying in the screams, wails, prayers; the howling of the stormy darkness; dispossessed shadows that cling to each other in fear; a song, unappeasable, unrelenting. . . In a night that even words cannot penetrate, the dawn you call upon is a dawn this world has not yet seen.

What was I doing there? But there was nothing left of an "I". . . No part of me could assume this pronoun, no part could face another and become one, not one part could shoulder a destiny or carry out a story to its end. I opened my eyes, found myself in a world of stone. The color of ash, of smoke, as gray as sorrow. . .

I closed my eyes, opened them again: I was still in the same place, in the same otherworldly truth. It was a nightmare and I was tumbling down, tumbling into its depths, trying to stop the freefall by grasping at whatever I could find, at times managing to stand on my feet, scars and bruises and all, but then falling down again. Whatever it was that had kept me on my feet, on this earth, in this body until this day had suddenly released me from its grip. In this desolate, entirely alien abyss, there was nothing, not even a single word, that I could hang on to, that I could sink my teeth or dig my nails into, to pull myself up and climb out. Even if I found something, could I hang onto it with these bare, dry hands, these broken teeth? My gums were still bleeding; I rolled the warm, bright fluid around my tongue. It oozed from the corner of my mouth, filled the back of my throat. If it just couldn't bear being stuck inside a frail, wasted body, the blood would have simply shot from my veins, but the way it was, it couldn't bring itself to desert me altogether. How long it took for blood to congeal. . . I wasn't in pain, nor did it taste as salty as they claim, but I just couldn't stop my jaws from chattering. Nothing is as bad as you fear, they say, those who don't know much about humankind, those who believe pain has a beginning and an end... Those who only circle the edge of a familiar abyss and are therefore never snared in the eternal noose of Horror... "Sooner or later, the sun rises," they say. And, besides, where else would we wait for daybreak if not at night? *Before daybreak you will betray me three times.*

### YOUR LAST PLACE OF REFUGE

You crawl over stones grey as humans, looking for a friendly hand, for a word to grab hold of and pull yourself up, for a river to carry you away. A river to quench your terrible thirst, a word, a hand... Groaning, trembling, your teeth chattering... You leave tracks along the wall — red, winding, fragrant roses that wither as soon as they bloom... You wish that you were dead, that you could turn into a winged creature, that you had never been born. That you had a God you could call out to and ask, Why have you forsaken me! Crawling on your knees and elbows, you desert your body as if it were a dry riverbed. You close your eyes to open them on a different world. A world that hasn't cooled, that hasn't even been created yet... Slowly, painfully, you move through the night

— always the same night — toward the window at the end of the wall, toward the strange, remote image of a face trapped in the cloudy glass. . . Spotty, disheveled, unmoored from time. Beyond your reflection lies the world outside, a blurry panorama. You approach it, drawn on by the ice-blue call of the pole star — it's your star now — that lies waiting on the horizon. You grasp the window ledge and slowly raise your body up, like a new moon rising over ruins. You want to ascend all the way to the sky — climb its airy stairs — turn yourself into a pale gold light and shine down on the night, on the dark waters, on people's long restless sleep, on the burnt forests of dreams. You can't distinguish the stone's darkness from the night's, the stone's night from the humans'. (Pegasus, created from Medusa's severed head, was born of the most ancient blood, the veins of marble. This is why the stars belong to the dead, why the faces of the lost ones are etched in the Milky Way. . .) Silently, you scan the world below, the wet, glistening rooftops, the streets that bear no trace of you or your absence, the public squares, the bridges, the jumbled, wavering lights of the city. . . The horizons that hold no promise other than new rounds of loss. Alone, painfully, you raise your body up, you stand beyond hope and despair, beyond good and evil, your exhausted arms limp like broken wings. Your last place of refuge. The recognition hits you like a blast of cold wind, eternity in the wind that blows through your hair, as if to make you whole again, piecing you back together, returning your face to you. Fingers of moonlight caress your eyes thirsty for sleep, showing you life as a miracle, then gently close your eyelids. Your body, immune to wounds now, quivers like a taut bowstring, standing at the earth's gate, awaiting its final banishment. It only takes two heartbeats — your journey from one horizon to the other; the morning star, your star, lets down the rope for you to climb all the way up to it; for the first time, acutely aware of your innocence, you lay your head down on the thorny night. Alone, defeated and proud, you lay claim to all the fates that converge here. Swaying quietly in the wind, standing fast in the middle of your own disappearance, you take responsibility for the lies of life and death. One more time, one last time, the magnificent song of the chorus is heard. It begins gently, expands, wave upon wave, rising beyond all the world's sounds and silences, beyond its skies and nights. "Don't stand back! Jump! Jump down!" Calling out to you, calling out to you and your solitude in your most authentic voice — that remote, improbably magnificent chorus, drums of victory or defeat, that wind. . . The wind.

∽

You thanked the stars, then died alone, mercilessly alone, on a starless morning, and, when your head fell in one swift motion, you brought the night to an end. For all of us. You had spread your wings too soon — on the stairs climbing up to the sky, on the very first stone step — you opened one wing to the light, one to the darkness. You lit the last candle of your strength, perhaps with a smile, offering it to the dawn. In that moment, a star was reborn. You left your eyes with me so that I can see life as a miracle.

# The Dreams

## THE ANGEL

We all saw the angel. At different times, in different places, on windy rooftops, in empty rooms, in corridors where no one walked. . . At a top floor window, calling out to the passing stars. . . Among the stones, having rejected his name, his fate, the ability to fly, waiting naked, helpless, ordinary. . . Alone, circling the abyss with his damaged smile, at the threshold of eternity. . . We saw him at daybreak, in the blood-red, fiery dawn hours, in a pure gold-colored light, in the sharp fluorescent light, in the raw light of a naked bulb, in impenetrable darkness. . . He flickered between being and not being, between the seen and the unseen, fading in and out. Some noticed only his uncombed, lion's mane of hair, some only his eyes shining like stars in his hollow face. None of us could look at him for long. Perhaps what we saw was a dancing shaft of light, or we just experienced him as a spring breeze, full of life and heavy with the scents of the red buds. That much was enough for us. The sound of a wing fluttering, a tiny little song, a memory flowering on its own, a few drops of rain. He had heard us and descended at once from the heavens, his hands and arms, his pockets full of letters, good tidings, promises, melodies. . . He had come bearing raindrops, rushing rivers, the surging waves of the open seas, far-off places. . . To some he had returned their childhood, to others he sounded the irresistible call of eternity. . . To some he had brought the smell of pine trees, to others the rustle of leaves. . . Some said he smelled like a wild animal, like wild roses, virgin forests, or the storm-battered sea, but above all he smelled human. He embraced each one of us, calmed us with the gentlest touch of his deft wings, with just a few tears. We could not have dreamed this up ourselves, because we had exhausted our dreams long ago. Had we come together — but we never did — we could have gathered his disparate images, here is yours, here is mine, and turned him into flesh and blood. We could have completed his interrupted story by adding sentences of our own, and we could have saved him. And then maybe we couldn't have. He was our lost one, lost forever, everything we had already lost and all that we would still yet lose.

Tired, depleted, he had taken on the ashen color of hunger, thirst, and isolation. He had his head on his knees, his hair hanging over his face. And yet, I thought I saw — if only for a moment — his eyes, incomparable, mysterious. . . He was made of an essence different from ours, made of the migrant moon and dreams, of silvery wings formed by the Milky Way, of verses not yet uttered, of a heaven the color of the heart. Of the deepest and most authentic Hell. His gaze, fixed on a point in the void, obliterated the void and replaced it with an entirely different, an altogether new universe. A universe yet unseen, yet uncooled. A universe I knew existed — alive, real, a universe that everything called forth, in which everything was made whole.

Bent double, seemingly in pain, he was shriveled, as if he no longer filled out his body. His clothes were torn, caked with soot and mud. The raindrops running down his drenched wings had formed puddles around his feet. From the heavens, from a place near the human heart, he had come rushing across this world's night from one end to the other, like he had started out too late. . . He had wandered in darkness, visiting our world, unsure whether he was hearing the living or the dead. He had come to live among us, stayed on with us, and he had been depleted. He had seen much, secrets, crimes, miracles, murders, the countless forks along the paths of being human. He had seen everything, seen himself in everything. He found less and less meaning in our world of voices and definitions; which is why he kept silent.

Suddenly lifting his head, like a puppet on a string, he jerked it back with a force almost enough to break his neck. His hair flung about, a ferocious laughter rang out. It was a terrifying laugh that came from the depths of the night, from the very depths, echoing, shattering against the walls. Savage, dazzling, free. This is how he revealed his mortal wounds. The cuts, bruises, burns — the crimson blossoms on our bodies — the dense forest of scars, the aimless river of blood frothing, brimming over, blood drying like wild roses. . . The wings he could no longer move. . . In that fleeting moment, unmeasurable by any measure of time, I saw that his face was covered in sweat — his face riven by the deep scar — a mask emptying itself out. . . Then his head hung down again, as if heavy with deaths — yours and mine — falling onto his knees. His vision splintered like old withered branches. The universe torn in two, streaming down like giant drapes to cloak his eyes, which he left with us. There, defeated and proud, with an extraordinary, superhuman exertion, he mustered the last traces of his strength and plunged into dreams.

**A.**

So this is the place they assigned to me, I have finally found the place I can call mine, where I can take root. Bare walls, a locked door that waits tensely, silently, this hollowed-out world of stone. . . This spacious void, this abundant emptiness, is my exile. They say that if you stare at the ceiling long enough without blinking, your entire past will appear there. A one-seat cinema where you can watch a film in which you are the main character. You can take it out of the canister, wipe off the dust, rewind it, and watch it over and over. Not because you love your life so much, certainly not the life that has been squeezed and squeezed in order to fit into this, the one that would spurt out if you stepped on it. . . But because you have nothing better to do. Is it easy to love a life that has been hollowed out? Especially when that life doesn't love me either, doesn't find me worthy of itself. Random gunfire, empty blanks; it's always someone else who dies, someone else who plays the part; curses, blows, insults come to an end, then start up again. . . dragging on like this. What past? I have no past! A soft flick and I free the bug that had lost its way among the shadows when it caught a whiff of human, the strange, bitter smell of a human. . . My gaze cuts through stones, layer upon layer of stones, it pierces through the roof, through the atmosphere, and, now free, it soars among the folds of darkness. It steals the night of the world. A new moon, groping its way forward, climbs in a spiral just beyond the horizon, searching distant corners for someone to call, to confide in, someone to console, to explain life's infinite vastness. . . But it calls to this world, not to us. I throw myself to the sky, my arms twine around the stars like ivy, I glide across The Archer, Leo with his mane, The Dragon, Pegasus with his broad wings, in this light, on this luminous trajectory, I become a comet dizzy with the fullness of infinity, chasing one dream after another, now The Hunter now The Argos, I grab hold of Libra's scales and, swinging, I leap from galaxy to galaxy, dissolving, dispersing in all directions. . . The Milky Way traces death's face, everchanging, deepening, flowering, in a tangle of branches. . . I stare for so long that my eyes become an ethereal, wayward light that loses its way and turns into the sky itself. It swells with rain clouds. The wind picks up, the storm begins, a star slips and falls. As if it had come to live among us and then lost its way back. Like a gift from God — I understand many things, but God is not among them. I pick up the star that has fallen from my night; wiping off the mud, I caress it gently, dress its wounds. But I cannot stop it from fading, from dying in terror. It crumbles like a twig in my battered hands — my fingernails have fallen off, my hands only know wounds, scabs, rope burns. . . They bind the hands of men like me so that we won't call out to death. Little beetle, how I wish that you hadn't come from the dark, or at least, for once, that you hadn't come for me! It did not move, perhaps it was playing dead. What can survive, once it falls into human hands! We finish what the earth and the sky have left unfinished. . . The club hurts, it burns wherever it lands but leaves no mark, deprives us even of a bruise. The strap is worse, it feels like a lightning bolt striking from within, tearing through your flesh. And the cane, it topples you like a tree, the shock quickly numbs you. But the next day, and the days that follow, the pain returns as if it had always been there, from the beginning. It returns with the southern winds, with the scent of the sea, melting snow, but the bones — time's white sharer of secrets — the bones endure. No one gets off easy, even an ounce of fate has its price. Pain is not as harrowing as they say, getting past it is almost a matter of arithmetic, you can't explain it or share it with anyone, not even with yourself, but once it's over, you forget it. Sooner or later you get some water or soup, a mattress, a stove, even watch a TV that still tells the same old story. I wish there was a blade of grass or a leaf between my teeth, the rush of a stream, rain falling on the sea. . . The world is what it is, but, hollowed out by the winds, it withers away, in time, it turns into a howl. Thankfully, no one notices. There is the asphalt that keeps you from seeing the earth, the earth and its dead. Walls, rooftops, ceilings, blind doors stretch like a curtain between the night's darkness and your own; streetlights illuminate hope's deceptions; legions of well-kept buildings, bridges, monuments rise between the stones' resolve and that of humans. Shortly before dawn, there is an hour when the night is over but daylight hasn't yet returned — the only hour when the city is entirely empty and quiet. The lights fade, everything hushes, even the pupils fall still under closed eyelids. And that is my hour. Alone, aimless, I walk the desolate streets, walk the pavements, the cobblestone roads of silence. The streets walk in me. Something calls to me, draws me out of myself, casts me far away; I shout with joy, sing, unfold my arms, whirl and whirl in the rain. Drops flow down my hair, my cheeks, from my eyes, rolling down my back, cleansing my heart, washing away the mud and the grime. Laughing, I bid farewell to everything. And if, just then, a tiny, wet, shivering bird were to perch on my shoulder, to tell of. . . the mischiefs and looting, of the other shores, the luminous sunrises of your childhood. . . Now this is a gift from God. I am thirsty but the door is opening, my only portal to tomorrow; soon the parade of hours and colors across the skies will begin. That's when they will take me upstairs, to the fifth floor.

## THE HEART OF THE LABYRINTH

Through the eerie twists and turns of the stone building, down secret corridors wrapped in a bluish haze, through one-way doors that open and close quickly, like turnstiles, you arrive at the heart of the labyrinth — impressive, real, hard as a fist. . . Here is a cold, empty room, white as a gravestone, no different from any of the countless locked rooms of the mind. This is where the voice comes from, the voice you hear in the deepest recesses of your being, the voice that speaks to you, hopelessly calls out to you. . . The place that you arrive each time you're swept along by that distant song, your solitude's companion, the song that weaves the roar of the wind and the humming of waves in seashells, the sailors' whistles and the spray of the ocean, farewell chanties and the beating of wings. After so many nights, so many dawns, so many lives you've left behind along the roads of this earth — sometimes overjoyed, taking in everything that came your way and adding it to your destiny, sometimes exhausted and falling apart, giving yourself over to everything that came your way, adding to its destiny — this is where you have arrived. No pillars, no statues, no echoes, the last room, silent through and through. . . The center of the labyrinth, its hollowed-out heart, where the Sphinx that falls into man's abyss will borrow your voice. . . The heart that beats in everything that has vanished or is not yet born, in everything lost or to be lost. . . Enveloped in this silence, you, too, can remain silent forever, waiting, watching over your death. You can invoke your most sincere prayer, your confession; you can freely shed the tears you've been holding back. In a room that has become your reflection, you stand still, turn your back and wait. Here you speak only the language of your blood, you scream, rebel, cry in despair. No one comes. All that's left is you the executioner and you the victim, face to face; and, maybe just to ward off the cold, you embrace and look into each other's eyes, like looking into the distance. Your tears fall, mingling, becoming a stream that follows its route to the soil, where, at the heart of the earth, it flows into its riverbed. Nine times it circles the world of the living, and then it, too, disappears.

When I saw him last, his head was bowed, as if he couldn't bear its weight. His hair covered his forehead and eyes. What frightened me most was that he might lift his head and look at me... What frightened me most... And what I most wanted: for him to look up, see me, murmur a word. A sign, a reproach, a farewell... He did none of these. This is how he left his eyes with me. Since he had no one else to leave them with.

**ME?**

What was I doing there? But there was nothing left of an "I"... No part of me could assume this pronoun, no part could face another and become one, not one part could shoulder a destiny or carry out a story to its end. I opened my eyes, found myself in a world of stone. The color of ash, of smoke as gray as sorrow... I closed my eyes, opened them again: I was still in the same place, in the same otherworldly truth. It was a nightmare and I was tumbling down, tumbling into its depths, trying to stop the freefall by grasping at whatever I could find, at times managing to stand on my feet, scars and bruises and all, but then falling down again. Whatever it was that had kept me on my feet, on this earth, in this body until this day had suddenly released me from its grip. In this desolate, entirely alien abyss, there was nothing, not even a single word, that I could hang on to, that I could sink my teeth or dig my nails into, to pull myself up and climb out. Even if I found something, could I hang onto it with these bare, dry hands, these broken teeth? My gums were still bleeding; I rolled the warm, bright fluid around my tongue. It oozed from the corner of my mouth, filled the back of my throat. If it just couldn't bear being stuck inside a frail, wasted body, the blood would have simply shot from my veins, but the way it was it couldn't bring itself to desert me altogether. How long it took for blood to congeal. . . I wasn't in pain, nor did it taste as salty as they claim, but I just couldn't stop my jaws from chattering. Nothing is as bad as you fear, they say, those who don't know much about humankind, those who believe pain has a beginning and an end. . . Those who only circle the edge of a familiar abyss and are therefore never snared in the eternal noose of Horror. . . "Sooner or later, the sun rises," they say. And, besides, where else could we wait for daybreak if not at night? *Before daybreak you will betray me three times.* I was trapped in an unbroken, eternal Now — the hour-hand had fallen off while the minute-hand circled endlessly. Hours, drenched in blood from endless whipping, could no longer pull their heavy load, neither a step forward nor backward, they could not budge Time. Didn't I already know that the world was filled to bursting with injustice, with tyranny? The world was miserable and dreadful enough even without these stones, these filthy, shameless cells, these doors opening to who knows where. Yet it was only here that the wire mesh fence around the courtyard was taller than a human being. *Before daybreak you will betray me three times. The first two times, you won't even know it. . .* The walls came closer and closer, becoming dark and alive, they closed in on me from all sides, trapping me in a body. The border between myself and my being hardened, even my voice could not pass through. My head on my knees, I waited to become a darkness indistinguishable from the night, or a dream woven from pure light. . . To take on wings, to turn into stone. I caught a whiff of my hair, the sudden sensation made me feel as if I had once been alive. Before I fell into pieces, into countless irreconcilable "I"s, from the savage terror that loomed like a sharp bone in the middle of my consciousness. . . As if I had lived once, before the earth's sleepless, exhausted cheeks collapsed into its ruined face. In this two-by-two and twenty-years-deep granite universe of mine, there was not even a corner left where I could curl up and breathe! A darkness closing in, taking shape and coming to life. A cold numbing my limbs cell by cell. Shadows, long dispossessed, thick as vapor. The tattered pillow of my lonely night. Voices, voices, voices. . . The taste of salt, of ash, lime, permeating the words. I began to braid my hair into thin plaits, pulling at my unruly mop, unable to divide it into three equal parts, twisting, weaving them together — like mooring myself in a secret internal harbor with flimsy ropes that unravel before doing their work — starting over, one more time, a second me, a third, patiently, as if weaving a basket where I can put flowers, on which I can rest my head and sleep. . .

In the beginning, I heard a gasping, stifled outcry. . . It stopped abruptly. Starting again, it turned into a wail — I could barely discern words within it. Then it turned into a sharp scream that wouldn't stop. . . Louder, resonant, echoing everywhere and in everything. A scream that pushed me back against the walls, into the furthest depths of darkness. With each passing moment, it felt more familiar yet no less alien, more intimate yet no less remote. . . As if the stones were trembling all around me, yelling, wallowing in agony. It wasn't clear whether the voice belonged to a living being, to a human or a creature much more innocent? To a body being strangled, or to the soul itself or to the Sphinx falling into man's abyss? The voice cuts out my heart with a dagger, hurls me to the nocturnal shores of terror, to the giant relentless waves coming from the deepest seas, destroying and drowning everything in their path and returning it back to the deepest seas.

Then, I recognized your voice, my own voice coming from you. How strange! What frightened me most was that you might cry, beg, collapse. You did none of these. As if death were some kind of overly dramatic end — a literary device kept on reserve for me. But you stood fast, suspended in the middle of a sentence where the dawn never arrives. The glow of your eyes the color of ash — the dull glow left by an extinguished star, by a cane shattered over bones, a rifle aimed at the ribcage. You lit the last candle of your strength and offered it to the break of day.

Perhaps even this stone world wouldn't withstand your cry much longer, your cry that swallows everyone and everything. It would crumble like a thin membrane, and, before it's my turn, become what it has been all along: ashes and dust. *Before it's my turn. . .* In the crashing storm confusing the earth and the sky, scattering my few remaining belongings to and fro — rags, broken syllables, letters — I had to quickly collect myself, save whatever I could, whatever was left of me. *Won't be easy.* I had to grasp onto my life, roll back the years in twos and threes, like threading a spool, and find a quiet heart to hide them in. With hurried steps back, from one beginning to the next, from daybreak to sunset, from memory to memory, from stone to stone. . . *When it's my turn.*

If I had a companion with me, I would have sown and gathered up the grains of the past, harvesting and offering them to him. I would have begged him to hold my hands, to let me rest my head on his chest and leave it there without saying a word. *Won't be easy.* I would have begged, cried, collapsed. Begged him to kill me, but to refuse to let me die; I would have cried and collapsed. If only I could look into a pair of eyes in the firmament, the all-seeing, all-forgiving dome of the sky, if I could hear the beating of a pair of wings, if only the wind could blow into the quiet corners, if only a leaf or a blade of grass were to appear among the stones to convince me of life's eternity. . .

Then, I recognized your voice, the voice of the nobody embodied in you. Thread by thread I weaved you from solitude, from my soul that they unraveled thread by thread, I gave you my name. Take it, please. Take this from ME. *Before daybreak you will betray me three times. The first two times, you won't even know it. . .* Until then you will wait here resting your head on your knees, among the screams, the curses, the stifled moans, the cries. As the braids in your hair come loose one by one. *It will be hard.* As in the dreams of stones, the lacerated bleeding stones. *Are you ready to fly?* I don't know. STRIP NAKED! Shed this body readily, your human condition wrought with shame, sorrow, pride, hope, and pain, from this vain anticipation you call my life, from all the magnificent words. . .

You thanked the stars, then died alone, mercilessly alone, and when the morning eclipsed the stars and your head fell in one swift motion, it was you who halted the night. You did it for all of us. You spread your wings much too early, on the first step of the stone stairs to the sky, opening one wing to the light, one to the darkness. You lit the last candle of your strength, perhaps with a smile, offering it to the dawn. In that moment, a star was reborn. You left your eyes with me so that I can see life as a miracle.

Sooner or later the night would come to an end, a dawn this world has never seen would break. Sooner or later the door would open, the litany of hours, of skies, of deserts in the skies would begin. Until then, I would be here awaiting my turn, blackened by boot scars, collapsing into a sleepless night with my head resting on my knees. I would wait for a story that has long forgotten me to come to its end... Wrapping myself in your fate, like retreating into the safety of a cocoon, I would wait for the time when I would take up the cry you left behind. The silence you left me with your last silent cry. *Are you ready to fly?* No, I'm not.

Who then was that voice that spoke with me, in my night? That spoke for all of us? Died for no one?

Your head had fallen. Covered in the wads of tissue they had plastered to your wounds, it was as if you had arrived at some strange blossoming. Your eyes were like two solitary stars concealed among the branches. You left them with me. I parted the branches one by one. Parted them for days and nights, for years. By the time I had finished, you were already long gone.

## THE DEAD

"They killed the angel. Up there, they took him to the fifth floor. . ."

"On his battered body, burn marks, fingerprint bruises, bootprints. . ."

"I heard that he wanted it. That he even begged, pleading, Kill me, let me die."

"He could have escaped, could have flown away if he'd wanted to. It was his choice. He came to live among us."

"His wings were broken. Broken on the hook, they hung him on the hook again, frail as he was, just like that. . ."

"He snatched a guard's rifle, I heard. But he put the barrel to his own head. He didn't know how to shoot, anyway!"

"If he wanted, he could have flown away, he chose to stay with us. . ."

"But he didn't!"

# The Laughter

A. never finished his story; the rings of hell are more twisted than a human life. Days passed, seasons were born anew, but he continued to trace circles that widened and contracted in the orbit of the stone building. He walked and walked, until he collapsed to the pavement from exhaustion. On the worn pathways of his life, on its nocturnal shores. . . He curled into a ball before doors that remained forever closed to him, in puddles of mud and piss, shivering in the cold. . . He talked and talked. . . Regardless of time, place, of

the living and unliving, laughing randomly, fitfully. . .
Sometimes he would fall down laughing, collect himself, then start laughing again, laughing until he was seized with spasms. He couldn't find anyone who'd listen. Perhaps the person who could hear his story, lend it meaning, complete it, was trapped forever inside the stone building. That's why A. learned to speak with the dead, with the birds, the wind. . . Sometimes, I'd catch him staring intently at the trash, looking for something long lost, something he knew was lost to him, something that had left no trace even among the castoffs and scattered waste of the world. Sometimes on an avenue, in the late morning, unaware that the day had already begun for other humans, lying on the pavement in front of a pudding vendor or an ice-cream peddler, like a statue that had fallen from its pedestal, motionless, sleeping. . . It seemed like he wasn't even breathing, as still as death, his fists always closed tight, as if he was hiding something, warming his last crust of bread or remnant of a dream in his palms. . . They would throw a bucket of water on him to wake him up and chase him away. He would return to the same avenue at night, sit in front of a glowing shop window, and turn from his view of the infinite

void, of his absolute freedom to let his gaze wander among the faces of the people. Like a ship leaving the harbor with all of its lights dimmed... He would hum a melody out of the corner of his mouth while he swayed to its rhythm, gently moving his shoulders, keeping the beat with his restless fingers. This voice, rising, halting, starting up again in another key, this dance that recalls a scarecrow swaying in the wind, the crystal darkness of his eyes shining like a moonlit desert — it was all so terrible! As if the skin of life had been peeled back from end to end, revealing the muscles, viscera, bones. The passers-by steered well clear of him, making a wide arc, and the halo of loneliness surrounding him grew darker and more dense, rendering him more and more invisible. Sometimes, when the time was right, he would smash the windows with one kick, climb into the display case, and pose like a Santa, a sultan, or a *sünnet* boy all dressed up in a general's costume, or like any mannequin he set his eyes on. He would take their clothes, wrap them around his head or neck, throw them over his back like a cloak, and rehearse like a thespian for his performance. Dignified as a prince returning from exile, he would sit on his magnificent throne among the garments and shards of glass, and begin his address to the people. As if he had finally decided to expose a secret, to put it where it belonged, in public view. His eyes blinded by the dazzling lights, he would begin that strange, formless narrative — his stark tale. . . A tale born of nothing — born of hungry hallucinations, the secrets of the stone, quietly closing wounds, the tale that had been erased at his birth. . . Not because he wanted to tell it, but because his tale had to finally take on a voice, words, a body. Then and there, among the bright colors, the soft fabrics, the flickering neon letters, the velvet curtains, the brand names: "Here, finally. They assigned me this place. In this hollowed-out world — luminous stars strewn everywhere — sweet-tempered stars —" he would say impatiently, hopelessly, knowing that he was running out of time. He would derive lofty — and unanticipated — inspiration from the mannequins, their naked bodies and fully attentive faces perfectly static, like brick walls. "One person is not enough to fill this world," he would continue, "there is a place for everyone. Come and see it for yourselves! The window is open. But I am the leading man. Am I everyman? I'm a common hero. I've sucked breast milk. And, can you tell, this is my stage voice." Then everyone would recognize A. who had crossed over the border between the seen and the unseen. A brief pause, a bewildered cry or laugh, and then he would carry on, full of disgust and pity. Weary of this cruel, primal spectacle of misery, weary of a destiny that evoked farce more than tragedy. . . At times, a child would watch him closely or try to imitate him, and that's when A. would become ecstatic, prancing back and forth among the broken glass in the mud-splattered display window. "This is your favorite place, isn't it? Your refuge!" Tracing a giant circle with his index finger, he started from his chest and then pointed to the shop-window, bringing it suddenly to life, then to the crowded streets, the distant watch towers of the city, on to the sky, his finger returning to point at his heart like a loaded gun. "I know this is your favorite place. But this is no place for humans anymore." "*He left his eyes with me!*" he would suddenly scream, with all the strength he could muster. Panting as if he were choking on his own voice, as if he was trying to swallow a stone lodged in his throat. He would grab at his chest as if trying to dig out his heart, the heart that had dragged him down these desolate roads;

and struggling to be heard, above all, by his heart, his voice would ring out: "Don't be afraid, I should have told myself. Don't be afraid, you won't die. Be patient, all of you, I'll die soon enough." Suddenly, he would realize that he was too late. He was too late for consolation. His voice gradually quieted, his thoughts became confused, and his shoulders slumped as he disappeared into a hazy halo that seemed to emanate from within. But he stayed upright and resumed his tale — that nobody quite understood — caught in the eternal gaze of eyeless mannequins the color of human skin, a gaze that rendered even Time utterly vulnerable. He would address the audience using the night's darkest words: "Who was there? Who emerged from the shadows and stood still? Who escaped, flew away with his one wing... Crimson flowers blossomed made of wads and wads of tissue, among the thick web of branches. You'd think the roots were in the earth, but they were in the sky. That's where we all come from." Holding a tired, bloodied heart — or perhaps a word, a breath or a wing — hidden between his palms, he would break it, like crushing lice between his fingernails. "They slit the moon in two as well, but it always comes back together."

In his borrowed kingdom, adorned with cloaks, epaulets and price-tags, he would pace across his life, from end to end, a life that was no less strange to him than it was to his spectators. He would struggle down the stone steps of memory, venture into tunnels no one had entered for a long time, search around in deserted rooms. At times, he would drop his story, lose it and thus arrive at his final place of refuge. And then his words would become entirely unintelligible. Returning to the universe that had sent him into exile, like a deity now, in a crown made of stars of his own night, he would become once more an accomplice to the crime of existence. He would take on all the lies of heaven and earth, all the murders, all the cries whose secrets he knew, he would lay claim to reality, to everything left behind by reality. But even reality couldn't afford to claim him. The extravagant dream that manifested itself, that no one wanted, that no one else had dreamt, would suddenly come to an end when the police arrived and dragged A. away. But he knew no fear anymore. He would resist, yell, scream, insist that he was the 'watchman'; he would complain of thieves, the thieves who had stolen his belongings, run off with his overcoat, his voice, his heart. But soon it was only muddy traces, an intense smell, and his dark laughter that remained in the jumbled shop window.

On the days that followed, at the translucent hour of dawn, I would see A. in front of the stone building; his shoelaces missing, his face black and blue, he had turned into a thick, impenetrable forest... He was calling to the birds, murmuring his song to the wind and the dead. Searching his hands for something, he could not remember what. His empty hands that had always managed to gather up and join the broken pieces of a life scarred into two unequal halves, pieces that would fall apart again every time. A. is a long, very long poem about human life. Long, unintelligible, unbroken. . . Perhaps interrupted by one misplaced verse, one hasty comma. A poem that no one understands or hears, thankfully, not even A. himself.

# The Stories

Surely, the man was telling the truth. He had been wronged; something that belonged to him was snatched from his hand, and he was subjected to violence for no reason. His absentmindedness, his gentle demeanor had been exploited; his trust was broken — trust in the streets he called home, in the people on the streets, even in youth as the very embodiment of innocence.

"The other one has the wallet. . . I am sure. I saw it with my own eyes. They ran in opposite directions."

He tried to mask his agitation, his anger, his strong, deep voice ringing with a metallic timbre through the crowded street. "Hurry! Don't let him get away. This is serious!" On the tall side, well-built, middle-aged, he was a good-looking man, even if he carried some extra weight. His self-confident manner, his understated, elegant suit, the personal touch evident from his scarf to his boots, everything about him made it clear that while he didn't belong in the back alleys, he was quite at home in them.

They stood on one of those dirty, noisy, brightly lit streets that had stopped being a back alley ten years ago by virtue of connecting two avenues. From one end to the other, the street was lined with *döner* stands, tobacco stores, nightclubs, beer halls (packed with customers standing at the bar, silently drinking and watching either the TV or the sidewalk), and then there were the new cafeterias with women in *Yemeni* headscarves kneading dough in the windows. A restless Friday-night crowd, indifferent to the rain, flowed left and right, bodies bumping into one another, making way for one another as if in a narrow hallway. Despite the blinding abundance of light, the showy, shining storefronts on every corner, despite the dazzling commotion that seized the night and hurled it away, casting it back to the sky, the street still seemed to possess a certain shadowiness. A certain odor that even the smell of freshly baked pita couldn't squelch, an odor that signaled a darkness waiting in ambush and evoked a sense of rot and decay... An essence of extinction, native to back alleys, oozing from the manholes, potholes and cracks...

The voice of self-control rang out once again with its metallic timbre: "He must know where his friend is hiding. You have to hurry!"

The man articulated his words one by one, as if speaking in capital letters, allowing sufficient time for each one to be heard. He emoted with the air of a lead character dutifully playing his part, even if it was rather ordinary or even boring... As if addressing the entire street, all streets, all human crowds, not just the police officer who was only two or three steps away... Untiring, he listed his lost belongings once again, giving all the details that he would no doubt be repeating who knows how many more times: passport, ID card, driver's license, credit cards... And he must certainly have incurred losses that were too private, too real to disclose... For instance, a number not saved to his cell phone, tucked deep into the corner of his wallet instead; or a black-and-white photo from when he was three years old; a good luck charm that protected him from life's mysteries; and a Libra pendant with a silver chain. A drop of cold sweat rolled down from his neck — who knows how long he'd had his coat unbuttoned — he realized he was shivering. That very same instant, he also acknowledged for the first time that he had been robbed; he felt helpless, used, stripped bare. . . It was as though, in addition to taking his wallet, they had even ripped off and stolen the pockets where he could have warmed his hands. Big, lofty words like Truth and Right, even Law, were on his side this time. Justice needed to bring the situation under control immediately.

The pickpocket was caught; the officer had his arms twisted behind his back, gripping the elbows tightly. He looked like he was twelve or thirteen. One of those kids who, though neither short nor skinny, always looked younger than they were, and who were ageless, with not a trace of childhood left in them. One of those who gave no clue about himself beyond what was demanded, and what was already apparent. . . His eyes were hidden, barely noticeable in his face that seemed swollen from the cold. Suddenly, he started bawling at the top of his lungs. More than a cry, his voice sounded like a slow, coarse, clumsy wail, a forced howl, a five-year-old's bad imitation of a bloodcurdling scream meant to aggravate an adult. . . As if the boy was trying to reenact a childhood he didn't really remember or believe in, to stage it before their eyes. . . Someone reached across his right shoulder and slapped him in the face: "Quit the act, kid!" It was simply a warning, a signal that more violent blows could follow; even so, the sound of the blow drowned out the street noise as the cop's fingers left their imprint on his bruised temple. The boy shut up immediately; lowering his eyes to the mud puddle, he didn't look up again. That's when he realized he had grown up. A melancholy expression too grave for his age settled on his face. A calm, hopeless sadness particular to adults, one that required years to harden and therefore appeared much more genuine on a child's face. . . A grief experienced for our sake. . .

"Didn't I tell you?" The self-assured voice rose again, convinced in its righteousness, expressing an emotion for the first time: pure, unadulterated hatred. "Of course he knows where his friend is hiding.

But we must hurry. He shouldn't get away." Probably, he wasn't aware himself of the amount of hatred he had for this world. . . As if he had been waiting for a long time to avenge himself on deceit and fate, suddenly seized with so much hatred. . .

The cop said nothing, giving another sharp twist to the pickpocket's arms, which were already twisted more tightly than was necessary. The boy wouldn't have run away on a street full of curious, mocking, and contemptuous bystanders crowding the corners and sidewalks. If anything, he had to adjust his stride to keep pace with his escort. He looked as if he were exhausted, on the one hand from the hatred raining onto him from all sides, on the other, from the oversized sorrow that had swallowed his frail body. . . From his long struggle to erase himself and live among people as a nobody. As if he'd walked through a time tunnel, he had aged even before reaching the end of the street.

"If he makes it to Tarlabaşı, you will never find him!" he insisted impatiently. The man had caught up with the cop, and was walking beside him with firm and resounding steps, in something like a spirit of teamwork. In the rain that was quickly turning to wet snow, the makeshift trio hurried on through the night, shoulder to shoulder, without looking around, feeling the northeast wind as they approached the three-way intersection.

"Don't worry! We'll take care of it," responded the cop eventually when they reached the intersection. . . He jostled the kid slightly as he gestured toward the dead end on the right. The last food kiosk vanished behind them; he hadn't eaten supper yet, and there were still three hours left in his shift.

"That's how they work. We'll figure it out!"

∽

"The woman spoke," said the stones to one another.

"The kid spoke." The kid didn't cry.

"The woman is crying," said the stones to one another.

"The angel died," they said. "No, he played dead."

∽

"Are you here?"

"Don't worry. We won't stay long."

"It won't be easy."

"Look at him. Do you recognize him?"

"When I saw him last, his head was bowed, like it was too heavy. What frightened me the most. . ."

"He left his eyes with me so that I could see life as a miracle."

"The voice that spoke to me at night, whose voice was it?"

"Then I recognized your voice, my own voice coming from you."

"The dawn always arrives, sooner or later."

"Take him, please. Take him from me."

"Is this your real name?"

"Scariest of all was when he would look up and stare at me."

"You will betray me three times before daybreak."

"Are you ready?"

"I don't know."

"You've come here before!"

"All of us — didn't we climb out of the same abyss!"

"Even so. . . I wish we were side by side."

"Don't cry!"

"Look at him! Look again! Do you recognize him now?"

"He left his eyes with me. Because he had no one else."

"Before it's my turn. . ."

"Are you ready to fly?"

"Don't be afraid!"

"Don't hesitate! Jump! Jump off!"

"That wind. . . The wind."

"In a night that even words cannot penetrate, the dawn you call upon is a dawn this world has not yet seen."

"Take this one to the fifth floor."

"You crawl on your belly over stones as grey as sorrow. . ."

"That's when the door would open, my only passage to tomorrow, the litany of hours, of skies, of the deserts in the skies would begin."

"I got thirsty."

"What business did you have with them!"

"But there was nothing left of an 'I'. . ."

"Even so. . . I wish we were side by side."

"In the same blood, in the same night, in the same cry."

"Is this his real name?"

"Before daybreak you will betray me three times. The first two times, you won't even know it. . ."

"Sooner or later, the night will end."

"Do what you will but do it fast."

"They didn't do much to me really."

"You can't take it!"

"Take it. Ride it out."

"You crawl on your belly over stones grey as humans. . ."

"Sooner or later, the night would end, a dawn this world has not yet seen would arrive."

"No one shows up."

"Then who was that voice speaking to me in my night?"

"Stones grey as sorrow."

"A scream that forces you to retreat into darkness, all the way back to the walls."

"Then I recognized your voice, the voice of Nobody coming from you."

"You halted the night. For all of us."

"On stones grey as humans. . ."

"He stood still, perhaps he played dead."

"They don't know what they are doing."

"What can survive, once it falls into human hands!"

"We can finish what the earth and the sky left unfinished."

"He denied it, so it's up to you."

"Because he had nobody to leave them with."

"Jump! I told you to jump off, pal!"

"That wind. . ."

"Recognizing his innocence with this much clarity for the first time. . ."

"You spread your wings much too early, one toward the light, one toward darkness."

"Is this his real name?"

"Don't cry!"

"Strip!"

"Didn't you recognize the man, you lay beneath him!"

"Your eyes were like two solitary stars."

"Then who was the voice that spoke to me? That spoke on behalf of all of us?"

"When it was my turn. . ."

"It is going to be difficult."

"Slut!"

"Why are you holding back! Shout!"

"Let me go."

"Don't be afraid, I should've said to myself. Don't be afraid, you won't die."

"The woman is crying."

"LIFE. In the name of that sumptuous alphabet feast, you struggle, you tell, you're changed, you tell."

"Did we want to tell?"

"Otherwise, what's the point of being human!"

"Nobody could hear, thankfully, not even him. . ."

"You stood still, in the middle of a sentence where the dawn never arrived. . ."

"He left us like this — unfinished, half-made, as we were. . ."

"He wanted it, I heard. Even begged for it. Kill me, he begged."

"Let me die."

"You left your eyes with me."

"Please take him. Take him from *me*."

"Then who was speaking for all of us?"

"The stones. . ."

"The wind."

"Are you afraid?"

"Don't cry!"

"Don't worry."

"We won't stay long."

"Who died for the sake of nobody?"

"Don't cry."

"When I was finished, you were already gone."

"Are you ready to fly?"

"No, I am not."

# The Endings

## THE END

We emerged like dreams in the translucent dawn, like gauzy, anxious shadows, the remains of the night. We left the stone building one by one. . . Like earthworms surfacing after a storm, confused, hungry, beat up. We were bursting with pain, shame, humiliation. . . We dispersed without speaking, without farewells, without even exchanging a glance. No one could bear to see their own eyes. . . To see the endless, the ever unending abyss in the other's eyes. . . We wished for one thing only: that our fates would never cross again; that even if we were to meet on a street, in a stone building, in a yard or a room full of corpses, we would not recognize one another.

We left shortly after daybreak, when the pale morning light was still colorless, before the day was claimed by crowds. We were small, diminished, weary. Like wrecks that had washed up on shore overnight during a roaring storm. . . Under the tense winter sky — a flat canvas stretched overhead — the outside world felt harsher, more frozen than the world we remembered. We were as free as the birds, as the wind, as the dead. . . Some among us turned and quickly walked away, stumbling like sleepwalkers, fading into the three-way intersections of the city. Some bent over and looked for a cigarette butt, as if hoping to light it up and get on with their lives crushed under heels. . . Some slumped on the sidewalk, like a stabbed, torn sandbag. Some pressed their parched lips to the wet pavement. To speak with the bare stones, to murmur or to shout at the soil hidden beneath the stones, to plumb the depths with their voices, to renounce their silence. . . To scratch, dig, claw through the earth's door, to hear if its giant heart was still beating. . .

Here we were, standing at the threshold of the new day, waiting in line at the door. Small, worn out, unwelcome. Like dark, broken halos fallen from the hands of some winged being in hurried flight to the morning star. . . We walked in a world that had become utterly unfamiliar to us, looking neither left nor right, our eyes turned toward the winter sun gleaming on the horizon like an ax, toward the sharp edges of all new days. Like mummies awakened after thousands of years, forced to harden up, to become human again. Time trailing from us in rags and tatters, smeared with the clay, the cold, and the nightmares from beneath. Forever one with disintegration and decay, the enigma at the world's core, eternal accomplice to the first — and neverending — murder. One with the river of blood that still and always runs. With the neverending disintegration of life itself. Split into selves who were strangers to one another, more deaf and lost, exiled back to the world of humans. We would call out, now from this side of the abyss, now from the other, sometimes we would stay quiet among the victims, somethines among the murderers. We would walk again, and once again, in the same tight circle, each time a bit more human.

But there was no new beginning in store for us, nor any consolation of starting over. No magic wand would want to touch our forehead; blood-sharpened knives would not cease to wound; in the future, there would be no doors opening to tomorrow, no one eager to listen. . . Betraying, we were betrayed by fate, by staying alive, by living; by winning the sole, the one terrible victory we had been defeated forever. Nothing compared to what we had been through, neither on earth nor in the sky. We didn't even have a language to tell the story, to give it meaning. Did we want to tell it? In these burnt ruins, where the ashes of guilt and innocence were mixed long ago, which cry could find its echo, an answer, an ending? Like a scratch that heals unnoticed, our cry had already faded from the scabby hands of time. In a world wrapped head to toe in whys and becauses and therefores, no sentence, no equation, no comparison had room enough for us, either. Like fallen letters from a word defeated by humans, it was as if each one of us was an 'E,' meaningless even side by side. Left behind by L-I-F-E when it fell from the highwire and broke into pieces, crashing on the rocks. . . Perhaps it was another word. . . One that clears its own way out of the night, laughing, singing, a word over which the day breaks.

Still. . . Had we been side by side. In the same night, in the same blood, in the same cry. . . Maybe we could have strung the letters together to express what had happened. Described the labyrinth, the labyrinth's empty, hollowed-out, heart, and the angel that appeared there, in a blurry mirror. We could have told the story, made it real by telling it. Real and immortal. We could have gathered up its wind-scattered images, joining them into a whole; with this from you, that from me, we could have given it flesh and blood. We could have completed his interrupted tale with sentences from ours, we could have saved him. A handful of hair, a huge nocturnal smile, a fragile body composed of all of us. A head bowed as if heavy. A humming song, a flowering memory, a few drops of rain, an ever distant sky. . . A handful of a starry void, a muted story. We could have found him a new word, a new name, a destiny with wings to fly. An entirely different end, beginnings that have yet to be invented. . . He could have echoed with our most silent cry; we could have become our most magnificent song. The song of Sirens pulling the human world onto the rocks... And perhaps we couldn't. Perhaps he was everything we had lost long ago, in the very abyss that we have become; perhaps we had lost everything from the beginning.

We couldn't do it. We each stood alone. In a different world, one that was more real or more imaginary, a different world yet unborn or long gone, we could have become the song... Shouldering the gravestones left behind by the night, we scattered into the visible world. No sooner had we arrived than we disappeared along the forking roads of the city, along the forked paths of the human soul, in its labyrinthine circles... We vanished, erased one by one in the daylight, like a dream no one saw, nor remembered or wanted...

In other parts of the world, in other continents, the night is just beginning, doors are being locked, shutters pulled down; alarms, whistles, and sirens warn the people of the dangers of the night.

## A.'S END

When I saw him last, his head was bowed, as if he couldn't bear its weight. His hair covered his forehead and eyes. What frightened me most was that he might lift his head and look at me... What frightened me most. . . And what I most wanted: for him to look up, see me, murmur a word. A sign, a reproach, a farewell. . . He did none of these. This is how he left his eyes with me. Since he had no one else to leave them with.

I look old and bedraggled, ancient as the world don't I? I'm past thirty now. I've been wandering alone, aimlessly, among ruins, on muddy roads, in deserted tunnels, on the cobblestone streets of life. . . I enter abandoned buildings, climb upstairs, appear in empty windows like a mugshot torn down the middle and taped back together, I climb the fire escapes, attics, roofs. I climb the vast emptiness of the sky, step by step, higher and higher each night, to the cliffs of human solitude. . . You need to be someone to keep on living; this is much easier on windy rooftops than among the stones. I look out over the earth's expanse to my heart's content, as if it were a resting place. I lift my head to the clouds, beyond the stratosphere, beyond reality, and embrace the wind. Quietly, I alight among the dead who whisper among themselves, far away from us. Fingers of vagabond moonlight linger avidly on my lips. Stars shine like a scream, dogs howl along the city walls, thousands of seagulls take flight, tracing circles. All things under the sky, those overlapping songs, played by a hollow reed, songs born anew of all that is or once was, all that lives and is yet to live. . . I heard him once, it's true, I heard him for the first time there; he was calling to the stars, to different worlds, all night long — talking to himself. I think I was jealous of him. The angel had shown me his wounds, laughing his strident laugh, dark as the night, he had shown me his mortal wounds. Perhaps he saw me, too. He had come to live among us, but then he left. And the song on everyone's lips had abandoned us, leaving us broken, diminished, weary, dissolving into all the voices, truths, and rages; only traces remained, like random feathers from birds in flight. . . We should gather it all together so that we don't lose him forever. This is the humans' task, to complete what the earth and the sky left unfinished. First one by one, then all together, it begins like a roar, crowds swell from the earth, rise steadily, rise in wave after wave. *Jump, jump off! Don't be afraid!* The cry wrests me from myself, hurls me into the air; I swing from one horizon to the other like a needle on a dial; like a feral dog on a chain, I hang suspended between earth and sky. . . But all things, even the heaviest, fly away in due time, as if on wings.

Sometimes, I look through the misty windows to see what's on the other side of the walls, the dark and somber doors. I look at the world — whoever named it so! — its veins visible beneath its wrinkled skin. My gaze lost in an ashen fog. People, more people, still others; they gather, speak, fall silent, each one lost in his own fog. Hands, faces, restless lips full of stories, decisions, judgments. Under the low, sturdy roof of their fiefdom, surrounded by posters, banners, mirrors, light bulbs, bathed in abundant light, they tell their stories at tables where they always sit hungry, though they never miss a meal. It's as if they have faced nothing but injustice but were never crushed, never surrendered or died. They jealously guard the bloated emptiness of their hearts. Surely, they are the ones with the right to live; death always visits others. It is always "him" who dies and walks away silently into the night. A couple of gunshots are heard from the TV, a demure cry declares how easy it is to kill in the midst of life's abundance; everything is an ordinary tale, a short film and nothing else — but I have no tales, tall or short! I watch people watching TV, their gaze is fixed, their faces are clear and untroubled; good and evil clash on a dazzling battlefield; voices, rage, ruckus, bargaining. They look at me as if they're looking in a mirror, aching, burning to see their own likeness in every mirror. And still, most of the time, even a whole person isn't enough to fill up their pupils. When everyone goes home — waiters empty the ashtrays, say a hasty goodbye to one another, turn off the lights — the owner of the café lets me in. I sit by the stove, the fire dies down, crackling, I finish the bitter tea left in the pot. I sit alone, silently, for hours, like the gatekeeper of a darkness that no one can enter or leave. I am forgotten here, locked inside myself. The night, already old in its first hour, approaches as if it's reaching for my body, suckling me with its cold, pitch-black, bitter milk. Insomnia, dreams seen with eyes open, I am their watchman, waiting. Waiting for everything to begin, to end.

Sometimes I wander among mounds of trash, among things that have been used and discarded by people, unrecognizable things, nameless, but even in this abundance, I can't find the word that's my share of it. In this world born of trash, of nothingness, one can find an arm, a leg, even a body, but not the word that has fallen from one's own darkness. A word with broken arms and wings, torn in two, ringing with laughter. Even if one were to find it, oh how hard it would have been to say it! My mind can grasp many things, but life is not among them. My hands understand life better than I do, perhaps this is why they remain silent like the silent scabs that cover them. Dreaming under these scabs, they are a companion to death more than life. Most have already been forgotten anyway, washed by rains, seeping into the soil; the dead and the living dwell in the same eternal sleep now. Shoulder to shoulder they passed through the night, the murderers and the murdered.

Still, it's not that bad. I find a half-eaten piece of bread or a *simit* beside me, maybe some rice left on a plate, I call to the birds. No matter what they say, birds are better than humans. Sometimes, if a bird perches on my shoulder, keeps me company, stays overnight... If a seagull with broken feet goes to sleep on my chest, while telling me about its childhood... Then, I feel like I might have a story of my own, too.

Shortly before dawn, there is an hour when the night is spent but the daylight hasn't yet returned — the only hour when the city is entirely emptied out; that is Nobody's hour. The sky is charged with signs, portents, births, it stirs restlessly in flames the color of blackberries, of pomegranates... I walk the streets alone, aimlessly — on muddy roads, on cobblestone streets of silence; the streets walk in me. I enter abandoned buildings, climb upstairs, appear in empty windows like a mugshot torn down the middle and taped back together; I climb the windy roofs. I slash my arms, my chest, my lips with a razor, not in order to feel pain — it doesn't hurt anyway — but to hear the blood roused from its sleep, flowing from the old wounds. The untamed blood surging from the heart washed by rains. Its voice is terrifying; it screams, howls, but it never lies. It never does. First one by one, they emerge from the cracks in the earth's crust; in ones and twos, then all together, a roar swells from the earth, rises in wave after wave. *Jump, jump off, scoundrel! Don't be afraid, you won't die!* The magnificent, incredible chorus that calls me to eternity, carries me, and escorts me on my journey. That always lies. . . Didn't we, all of us humans, spring from the same abyss? Tomorrow, when the pain returns, it will have changed into something else, into life's black-and-blue fingerprints, into a past that belongs to me. It's good for a human being to have a past, to be able to tell his great story in the past tense.

Otherwise, what is a human being! Just futile laughter.

# Epilogue

Somehow, what frightened me most was that he might cry, beg, collapse. He did none of these. When I saw him last, his head was bowed as if weighed down with all the deaths, he sat like a statue that had been watching the desert with its worn-out gaze for thousands of years, utterly alone, abandoned. Bent double as if in pain, he was a shriveled mass, shrunken inside his clothes. His hair fell over his face, covering the old scythe-shaped scar he secretly cherished. I don't know whether he saw me or not; he didn't raise his head to look at me. (How I wanted him to look deep into my eyes, to look into those depths where my true self had hidden, but this was also what terrified me most...) Perhaps he sensed my presence like a breeze that lightly ruffled his hair and caressed his forehead, like a timid ghost, a short dream, a memory. Years had to pass for the truth — which I wouldn't have recognized in that moment's icy claws — to dissolve and seep into my consciousness. That this was a farewell that would last a lifetime, final and irrevocable, one that would shield me from everything... The other me he saw — more alive, more genuine, more imaginative, that once-and-never-again self, defined by the range of his gaze and his lifetime — vanished forever with him. I, on the other hand, went on living, diminished, weary, carrying my dead self inside.

He believed that murderers were trapped forever in the icy stare of their victims. Like flies trapped in amber, unchanging over millions of years. Caught in their own murder. Like a two-dimensional, still, frozen image in a universe whose light is swiftly dying out... Like a speck, steadily diminishing, in that last stare ascending to the sky, wrapping the earth in its vast universe, in the endless infinitude of time. Perhaps this is how he leaves his eyes with me, returns me back to life, drawing me out from that dark, absolute, eternal unchanging universe. L-I-F-E. Didn't we stay alive for the sake of this magnificent feast of letters!

For the sake of that magnificent feast you struggle, speak, change, you achieve. Taking on the strength of another, of another you, you overcome this world's night. You survive on strength borrowed from the future; you keep moving toward the new day, toward the sharp edges of all new days. But your night makes it to the other side of the horizon long before you do. Up and down, you pace your memory's endless, shadowy hallways, you climb up and down its stone stairs, enter empty rooms, wait and listen. Sometimes, in the silence of a stone or a human face, by a noose hanging in the forest or on the gallows, you trace circles that expand and contract. Like a voiceless scream, like a word denied its syllables, like a half-erased verse, you wander on life's worn-out trails, its dark shores. There is the asphalt, you can't see the soil or the bodies beneath it; walls, ceilings, blind doors stretch like curtains between the night's darkness and yours; streetlights illuminate the deceptions of hope; immense flawless structures, buildings, bridges, monuments, stretch to the cliffs of your solitude. Splitting into a multitude of selves — more distant, more deaf and lost to each other — you begin the same exile again and again, each time a bit more human. You circle the abyss, calling from cliff to cliff, falling silent now among the dead now among the living. You are the mugshot torn in two and taped back together, crowned with the stars of your own night, you search for the path that will take you back to yourself, where you came from. Far from the secrets, the crimes and confessions, you search for the pathways of your blood, the door of your heart. There is a graveyard steadily expanding inside of you; you visit less and less, each time quicker to turn back and leave in defeat. You hold a spent word in your hand, shake off its dust, press it to your ear. You call to it, you yell through it, you fling it into the air like a dead bird. You climb to the rooftops of the round, drowsy world of humans, look out at the streets, horizons, the distances that carry no trace of you. This is the entirety of your final place of refuge! A frosty wind against your face, a faraway sky, an emptiness with a few stars, a small precipice. The sound of a wing. You are still alive. There, just like that, suspended, waiting, swinging back and forth like a needle between the earth and the sky, almost like being suspended between being and nothingness. . . You sense that your two selves — the alive and the dead — call hopelessly to each other; each one a victim of the other's abyss, calling out, always calling out without ever being heard. . .

As for me. . . Each time, I explained myself incompletely, incorrectly. In the wrong place, at the wrong time. Resorting to a language that was either too dry or too tragic. . . I strung together four, five hollow words, as dreadful as a skeleton, speaking in unyielding silences, in words more muted than spoken. Or, as if life was suddenly demanding to be narrated, described, expressed, I spouted lifeless metaphors, verbs stretched tight as a bowstring, images in search of their true forms. Until I had no strength left. I wandered among the walls of words, row after row, groping my way forward; like an apparition in the moonlight, I entered my story uninvited. A story that is no less unfamiliar even to me — my makeshift, formless story. . . Hollowed-out, worn away by winds, covered in sand and rainwater at birth. . . There, among the rugged stones piled one atop another, in a place where no one would approach me, I stood alone — naked, lost, defeated to the end. Far beyond tragedies, beyond crime and mercy, my fate unraveled, thread by thread, letter by letter; I dissolved in the churning muck. Unable to find the word that could bring me back to myself and free me from him. A word that had survived the blows of thousands of years, still intact, its limbs unbroken, a word that emerges from darkness able to usher in a new day. I spoke behind masks that sometimes smiled, sometimes cried; I spoke of what became unspeakable as I spoke; like a shadow, I followed their whispers, tears, and screams. I sent some of them to the streets, some to the stars, some to silence. The only one who could have brought my story to an end — my story that even truth no longer claimed — the only person who could make it mine and return it to LIFE, where it really belonged, had vanished long ago. Only life could confirm, lay claim to, and bear up what had transpired. There was not a single word that remained, no word that didn't crumble like a dry twig in my hands, that wasn't a witness to my darkness, that didn't bleed in my silence.

But sometimes, very rarely, I hear a voice inside myself that doesn't resemble mine — a voice that is neither human, nor does it speak to humans. I hear my blood awakening, flowing through the old wounds, bursting from open veins... And the screams roused by the oldest, truest fears, I hear them, I remember how they were screamed in order to stay alive. My wounds speak very rarely and never lie. But even their incoherent, dreadful sound shatters against the inscrutable walls of the human face and speech, turning into lies and falling to the ground like rain. That voice loses its way among the circles, detours, cul-de-sacs of a labyrinth, dissolving into thin air without meeting a single heart.

I think I call to the dead sometimes, sometimes to life itself. Which one answers or will answer, I don't know. But sometimes, when a song that one of my scabbed-over selves begins to hum for no reason reaches all the way to my heart, in all its clarity and wholeness, I recognize this voice that comes from the depths of the earth or the sky, I remember once thinking it was mine. That song born of nothingness and reborn in everything, the one that steadily grows and spreads wave after wave, I understand that I still hear it, always hear it. A song that grows louder with every human being on its path, crosses beyond horizons, reaching for its intended destination, an unclaimed heart, the heart of Nobody. Toward the pit where all disappear. . . Born from an interminable cry as it was from an angelic, dark laughter, as much from life as from what was not lived. . . A song of what has been lost and will be lost, of sunlight and stardust, of dreams the color of the human heart, of first and last glances, of distances and of the nearby, of farewells that last a lifetime, of gallows, winds, rocks, elegies; of rain that falls on water, runs through the soil, fills the eyes; a song of everything unsaid even when said. . . But of course, I always join the song in the wrong place and in the wrong key.

Your head had fallen. You seemed to be achieving a strange blossoming amidst the wads of tissue they had applied to your wounds. Your eyes were like two solitary stars concealed among the branches. You left them with me. I parted the branches one by one. Parted them for days and nights, for years. By the time I had finished, you were already long gone.